Parcel o' Rogues

Gordon Lang

Books by Gordon Lang:

The Carnoustie Effect/Warfare in the 21st Century
For Führer, Folk and Fatherland
The Giftie
The Half Sister
The Nazi Gene

(In German):

Die Polen Verprügeln, Vols. 1 & 2
Das Perestrojanische Pferd

The right of Gordon Lang to be identified as the author of this work has been asserted by him in accordance with the Copyright, Designs and Patents Act 1988

Gordon Lang
Parcel o' Rogues
© 2013 Conflict Books, London E3
All rights reserved
Printed in the UK 2013 by anchorprint.co.uk
ISBN 978-0-9558240-2-9

The Lion's Mouth, by Dr Alasdair Bruce, is published in these pages posthumously. The manuscript came to light only after the doctor's body was found, in what are usually described as mysterious circumstances, on a railway line near Helensburgh.
Officially, his death was recorded as suicide...

PARCEL O' ROGUES

I

CORPSES are all right, provided they are still in one piece. Tidy, like the ones on the dissecting tables in films. It is the bitty ones that cause all the trouble.

A body sliced randomly into seventy-one pieces is a bewildering sight. It is hard at first to believe that all those fragments have come from only one person. There is just one way to be sure that no more than one poor devil is on the table: hold an inventory of hands, feet and other bits – what is left of them – then bite the bullet and get on with the jigsaw.

I was involved in a case once – better that I don't give any details – where all there was to identify a body was a brass belt buckle. This was a Cold War matter, and we had to be certain that the other side had not simply made our chap disappear and left the buckle to fox us. As it happened, we were able to make quite sure that this was not the case, and there was no harm done. Except of course to the wearer of the buckle.

To step out in front of a train, though – is that what you and I would do? It must be quick, admittedly – damned near instantaneous – yet what a mess to leave behind for relatives who have to carry out an identification!

Goodness knows what goes through the minds of relatives who are asked to identify a person not from the body itself but by means of some artefact such as a ring or a wristwatch.

Officials must have an entertaining time devising imaginative fibs for the delicately minded. On the other hand, I do not doubt that most family members are not fooled, and make their own willing contribution to the kidding game. This is, after all, a simple matter of emotional self-defence. We cannot let ourselves think the unthinkable.

In the present instance, the dead man was identified tentatively from documents in his pockets and, later, positively from fingerprints. It turned out that he was a hospital registrar. The question was the usual one: Had he stepped onto the railway line voluntarily, or had he been pushed?

I had nothing to do with the case at that early stage. It was long after the official investigations were concluded that I came in at all. And if I hadn't broken my neck I should never have been involved even then.

My broken neck was a massive joke. After all the opportunities that I had given the Iron Curtain lot to snap the relevant vertebrae – chances that had mysteriously been spurned – I had to do the job myself by tripping over my own feet.

The break had not healed, and I stood there now, calloused ends of fractured bone clicking away merrily from time to time, waiting for two men who were on their way with a van full of explosives and the determination that somebody or other would die.

I had a bullet in me, too, but had not collected that until last night, and it wasn't doing any harm simply in a shoulder. I was bleeding a bit, though, and should have to have it taken out as soon as tonight's business was over.

I was neatly tucked into a corner full of shadow, in the angle between two walls. People could walk past me and not notice that I was there. One or two did go by, but not very many. This was a windy spot, and mid-September is not the most inviting time of year for late-night strolls in Scotland.

About the two men who were heading my way with explosives I knew next to nothing. They knew even less about me. They believed me to be dead. They thought that they had killed me with a very clever piece of technology, something that the public at large would not believe to be possible.

That had been the last of three attempts to put me out of the way. Tonight I was going to put *them* out of the way. With no mistakes.

I knew what the men looked like, and had the Christian name of one. I knew their plan, and that was enough. There had been a couple of schemes belonging to the madmen's plot that I had managed to prevent. All I had to do now was to foil the big explosion. Political murderers were damned well not going to succeed in my country, if I could do anything about it. We'd had enough of that with Cromwell.

It began to rain and, as only to be expected, the wind blew plenty of water directly on to me in my corner. Ears programmed for the sound of a van, I went again in my mind over the succession of events that had led to my being here now.

Without Major Jardine (now Lieutenant-Colonel), I should never have found out anything at all about the plot. The sturdy and unflappable Jardine, with whom I had served during that recent shooting match on

9

Craigard, had recently become a father. On the point of receiving his promotion, he was waiting at home on leave before taking over command of an infantry battalion in the South of England.

It was a bonus accruing from our brief spell of action together that Jardine had invited me to visit him and his new family.

I enjoyed the drive from Argyll. It took me through so many landscapes that were familiar yet every one possessed of that magical Highland power to surprise. Drive along those roads as often as one liked, and almost every time one could discover fresh lights and colours one had never seen before.

It was noon when I pulled up outside the house whose whereabouts Jardine had described to me in unmistakable detail. I sprang out of the car, locked it, dropped the keys into a jacket pocket and started towards the house clutching the parcel that I had brought for the Jardines' baby boy.

Something like a dozen paces were all that were necessary to reach the door of the house. The way was concreted and perfectly flat. What happened next I can describe but not explain. Just over halfway to the door I found myself stumbling over nothing at all.

There was no step or other possible impediment to orderly progress. Yet there I was, tripping the heavy fantastic, flying forward head first a couple of feet above the ground, just as I had done years earlier, tackling those beggars on the other side when I was a rugby three-quarter.

One is never too old to do something silly, that was clear. The crack when I hit the wall of the house with the top of my head was a reminder of all the other such blows my cranium had sustained from boyhood onwards. I had forgotten just how those shocks felt, had never expected to experience one again. The collision with the wall bent my head backwards, and I knew that my neck was broken. Despite the almighty crack of skull against stone wall, my head did not hurt. It was my neck that told me it was in trouble.

That's all there was to it. Well, not quite all. Lying there flat, face buried into a well-packed flowerbed, I was aware that only one limb – my right arm – still had movement. Both legs refused to be wiggled, and if I had any idea of turning myself over, that foundered on a left arm that felt literally dead.

Oh well, I could still do pistol shooting and fencing from a wheelchair. Play table tennis, too. Could my E-Type be adapted to give me automatic gear change? Though it does seem almost sacrilegious, a few had been built that way, I know. With the desecration of a gear change adaptation, I should have no difficulty at all in driving one-handed.

I had already had plenty of practice at that sort of thing. More than once I had driven in excess of a thousand miles across the Continent with an arm dangling uselessly. That had been more difficult, since each time I had been in a left-hand drive German car, with my right arm out of action. This had meant reaching across with my left hand to a gear change in the middle. I had done that without difficulty. How much simpler it would be in my right-hand drive two-seater, with only my left arm *hors de combat*.

There was just one potential awkwardness. If I did not regain use of my legs, I should need some adaptations to replace the car's pedals.

I certainly did not want to relinquish the Jaguar. It had been the car in which Anna and I had driven on our honeymoon tour. It was forever bound up with memories of Anna, and I intended keeping it going for the rest of my life – or for as long as I could continue to drive, anyway.

During my years at Berlin Station, the E-Type had remained in my mother's garage at home in Argyll. The last thing that was needed in the Service was a car that would attract attention. The Jaguar was an indulgence kept for leaves at home, and as a reward to savour in my retirement years. Consequently, she had few miles behind her, and remained in superb fettle. There was an F-Type out now, of course, and naturally she offered a range of technical advances. All the same, the E-Type was my car, and I was not going to part from her.

I ran through all these thoughts by the time Jardine opened his house door. Before any of them, though, my first notion had been the reflection that probably only another half inch or so would have sufficed to snap not just a vertebra but the spinal cord as well. It would have been an easier exit from life than my poor Anna had endured.

Jardine had heard, then seen, the arrival of my E-Type. When he opened the house door, he tells me, all he saw at first was the parcel that I had brought for his baby. This had shot out of my hands, rocketed against the door and fallen to the concrete. I was at first not visible to him, lying as I was to one side of the doorway.

Jardine's reaction on seeing how I lay was to attempt to give me ease by prising my head away from the wall of the house. I am sorry to say that I had to shout at the poor man to leave my head alone and call the professionals. Jardine could not know what I did about my neck.

In no time, the ambulance service was there – a vehicle crewed by two extremely competent women who trussed my neck in a neat figure of eight before rolling me onto my back and enlisting Jardine's help in lifting me into their vehicle.

It would be pleasant to record that from that point on, the attention of everyone in the medical services was of the same admirable standard. Rather, the first efforts of the National Health Service staff at the local hospital were seemingly aimed at ending my life.

II

I HAD never heard of the Liverpool Pathway. I simply went along it. Not all the way, of course. The so-called pathway was a system, evolved apparently at Liverpool, whereby medical staff concluded that a patient was dying and eased him on his way.

I was not dying, confound it, but somebody must have decided that it wasn't worth while trying to save me. Quite a few people who have known me might well have thought – and still think – the same, and we are all entitled to our opinions. My value or otherwise as a human being aside, I was not dying. Hospital staff set me along the pathway just the same. Apparently the Liverpool technique consisted chiefly of sedation and dehydration. Not that I was aware of what was happening. All I knew was that I was enjoying the most fantastic hallucinations (evidently induced by drugs I had been given) and was as thirsty as hell. There was no way of asking for a drink, since the bell push normally found beside each bed had been looped up out of my reach. I had been deposited in a small side room where I could see no windows, and where there was no other occupant or staff. All on my Jack Jones, I was left literally to fade away.

As for the end of the story, the best I can say is that a funny thing happened to me on my way to Liverpool. The funny thing consisted of the intervention of Britain's newest Lieutenant-Colonel.

'I have had no training, you understand', Jardine explained to me later. 'I learned bits and pieces about it by watching Naismith and his medics in action'.

Captain Naismith was the medical officer on Craigard.

'What on earth could you learn about medicine just by watching?'

'About medicine, nothing. About patient care, though, enough to sail right in, all guns blazing. I gave them hell about your call button being out of reach. Where, I wanted to know, was your water? Why did you have no drip? They tried to kid me that everything was all right, but I knew a little too much, in particular about dehydration. That is an absolutely horrible way to let someone die. I demanded water and told them that I should sit by your bedside all through the night – in fact, all through every day and night if necessary'.

That I could well picture. Good-natured Jardine, the coolest man in an emergency that I had ever met, could be fearsome when it was called for.

'You certainly seemed to be there a lot', I remembered. 'Every time I opened my eyes, there you were. What about wife and baby?'

'Oh, my wife's sister was there to lend a hand, as you would have seen had you made it through our door instead of trying to head-butt your way in through the wall. Anyway, it was only a couple of nights that I needed to stick around. Then I wore the people in that place down and they moved you into a proper ward'.

'And I thought everyone was jolly good'.

'They were good, on the ward. They were a different set of people altogether. I never again saw any of that lot that had put you into the side room'.

'I can't remember any of them'.

16

'You wouldn't. They were just keeping out of your way and leaving you to snuff it quietly'.

'And all I knew of it was being ridiculously thirsty. Plus of course those amazing hallucinations'.

'Somebody somewhere evidently thought that you weren't going to make it. Or even if you did make it, you would be useless, without the use of your limbs'.

'The legs came back after a few days, and then the arm followed. Anyway, even if I had been left with only the one arm, I should have made out all right. I was lucky, I know, but what on earth made anyone think that I should not survive?'

'When I saw how they had abandoned you to perish, I was damned angry, I can tell you. Because you were drugged up to the eyebrows, you weren't aware of the situation'.

Well, I certainly remembered the little room, and cursing heartily at the lack of water. Death by dehydration, and done deliberately. I could never have imagined such a thing. Certainly not from what is called our 'health' service. Even the very worst criminals in prison, I remember telling myself, would be given water. Still, I have to admit to one thing that the Liverpool pathway enthusiasts had understood properly: there was no one whom my death would inconvenience. Wife dead, mother dead, my only relatives a few cousins and a couple of ancient aunts from whom Service life had long since estranged me.

Even so, the laugh was on those who thought that I was on my way out. It was also on me. As though tripping over my own feet were not joke enough, there were two more ironies to come.

17

First, the snapped vertebra refused to heal. This paid me back well for my damned know-it-all cockiness. Having broken a good number of bones over the years, including two other vertebrae well below my neck, I had convinced myself that I could always tell when a fracture had healed. Two weeks into lying in a hospital bed with a cast-iron apparatus holding head and shoulders rigidly together to prevent neck movement, I announced that the cervical break had knitted. I could feel how solid the bone was now.

A fat lot I knew! A further four weeks after that, x-rays revealed that the break had not healed at all. A surgeon might be able to do something about it. Otherwise, I was to live the rest of my days with a broken neck.

And damned lucky I was, too. Lucky of course that the spinal cord, though damaged, had not snapped.

The second joke concerned what I had been foolish enough to think was going to be my retirement. In a vague sort of way I had been entertaining a vision of peace-filled days troubled only by the need to avoid bumping my head too hard.

I could not have anticipated the seventy-one piece doctor. He was the first victim of the men I was waiting for now, the duo with the van full of explosives. They had killed him on no more than suspicion that he had found out about their plot. They could not be certain, but the pair were fanatics, and fanaticism is inimical to evidence and reason. As I thought about this, the hand in my pocket tightened in reflex action around the means that I was going to use to stop them and to avenge the young doctor.

III

WHILE the doctor was still in one piece, I had known the man. His name was Dr Alasdair Bruce, and he was a registrar on my ward. Tall and slim, with curly brown hair and wearing metal-framed glasses, Dr Bruce had been a regular caller at my bedside.

Our first meeting came when they finally abandoned expectations of my death and shipped me from the dying room to his ward. It took several days for my mind to settle down from the bedlam of drug-induced hallucinations that I brought with me from the Liverpool pathway. At critical moments, Dr Bruce seemed always to be on hand. Over the next weeks, I found the young doctor charming, helpful and engagingly studious.

It was the junction between the top two cervical vertebrae that I had broken, he explained – the most complicated joint in the spine, allowing the head to move up and down as well as from side to side. God had joined, and I like an idiot put asunder.

It appears that this is a break one is not expected to survive. I was even luckier than I had thought, and once I knew about this, the Liverpool Pathway ceased to seem so unreasonable.

Having meanwhile become familiar with the almost round-the-clock routine of the hospital, I was not surprised when a porter arrived late one night to take me away in a wheelchair. The consultant, I thought, must want more x-rays.

Instead of to the x-ray department, the porter took me to a room with only one bed, like the one where I had been left to die. No effort was made to put me into the bed in this room. It was already occupied, by a man with greying hair and the purple face of a drinker. He was not drunk, but was delirious. I supposed that when I was suffering hallucinations I must have acted like that. The registrar, young Dr Bruce, was with the patient, and obviously very concerned. He took my wheelchair from the porter as soon as we arrived and sent the porter away.

I saw that the name over the bed was Simon Grant. The patient was rambling, in a very agitated fashion. He addressed Dr Bruce, who sat down close to the bed, crouched over to catch every word, as 'Bruce'. It took me several minutes before I realized that the delirious Grant was mistaking the doctor for an intimate friend.

'Leave the monument alone. Just concentrate on the castle', were the first coherent words that I was able to pick up from the man's delirium. Meant nothing to me.

Grant beckoned. 'Bruce, Bruce', he said, switching to confidential mode. 'Come closer'.

The doctor was already sitting as close to the bed as was physically possible. He could move closer only by rising from his chair and leaning over so that Grant's lips all but brushed his ear.

What followed were not subdued whisperings but a fragmented series of what seemed like excited sales talks. Whether Dr Bruce followed any connection in the content, I did not know. I myself caught only phrases that meant nothing. 'All worked out'. 'Fits beautifully'. 'Doesn't matter'. 'Dynamite'. 'It will be too late'.

After a pause that seemed to indicate exhaustion, the man in the bed tried to sit up. He managed only halfway before a final emphatic pronouncement: 'Those blasted Poles. We'll show 'em'.

The last that I heard was the patient's chuckle. Then Grant closed his eyes and was silent. Dr Bruce placed an ear close to the man's nose, and I realized that he was checking for breathing. This was, after all, a dying room – for all I knew the same dying room where I had been left.

The doctor straightened up, seized the handles of my wheelchair, whirled me round and set off down a series of corridors without calling for a porter to take me from him. He stopped at a small office, pushed me inside and closed the door.

'Did you understand any of that?'

'Only odd words'.

'That man is mixed up in something nasty, and I've still no idea what it is. I'm sorry to drag you in. It's only because I've read both of your books that I believe you can help. If you can make any sense of what he was trying to tell me...'

Just as long as he didn't think that I could work miracles.

The doctor spread his hands. 'I know you retired early, and I really shouldn't ask you to do anything, but frankly I don't think I'll have very much longer to get anything out of the man. He's sleeping now, but he'll die within a couple of days'.

'What's killing him?'

'Internal injuries. Car accident. We can do nothing'.

'He's doped up?'

'To some extent, yes. Strong painkillers, of course'.

'Including hallucinatory ones?' Wasn't it painkillers that had sent my own mind tumbling into a haywire world of fantasy images?

'There was no evidence of hallucinations. In front of any of the other doctors, no talk of those intriguing things he's disclosing now, either. He didn't open up until he saw me alone, and I was seated by his bed. I noticed that he gave me a sharp look once he heard me addressed as Bruce. It was as though he were seeing me for the first time, and from then on it seemed as though he couldn't wait for us to be alone together. My guess is that I must resemble – roughly – a friend of his called Bruce who wears glasses just like mine and looks roughly the same'.

It had long been a conviction of mine that good doctors were possessed of sharp sight, that they gathered a great deal about a person simply through a keen look at him. I had observed this facility in several physicians. It was what Dr Joseph Bell had been trying to teach his medical students at Edinburgh University with those words that one of them, Dr Arthur Conan Doyle, made so memorable for us: *You see, but you do not observe.*

Dr Bruce knew how to observe, that was patent. I had seen the trusting way in which Grant spoke to him, and had no doubt that the doctor had his patient correctly weighed up. I had not noticed at the time, but it struck me now, that the doctor had positioned me in my wheelchair so that the man in the bed could not see me. So far as Grant was concerned, he had been talking to Bruce alone.

'What visitors has he had?' I wanted to know.

'Only two men, I am told. I have not seen them myself, and the nurses say that there have been no others'.

'Only men? No woman at all?'

'He's a widower, apparently, without children'.

'What do you think he means by Poles?'

'No idea'.

'Any Poles visit him?'

'Not as far as I know'.

'Letters from Poland?'

'No one has mentioned any. Could have been a topic of conversation if there had been'.

'The men who came – are they relatives?'

'It seems not. They told us they were friends'.

'Friends. And it is with these that he is mixed up in something nasty?'

'It looks like it. He lives alone and we have no address for any relative. His accident was reported on Scottish Television news as well as in the papers, and only those two responded to it by coming in to see him. It seems reasonable to assume that they have a close relationship'.

I could only agree. 'First thing', I told the doctor now, 'we'd better pool whatever we made out from what Grant was trying to say. Then we can decide whether it has any value or is just imagination on his part. Where do Poles come in? Have you any idea?'

'Not the least'. The doctor had out a notebook and pen. 'If you can tell me everything that you understood, we'll see what tallies'.

It was a disappointment. I had been able to catch little, and could add nothing to what Dr Bruce had recorded.

'From that lot', said the doctor, 'you'll be wondering why on earth I believe that the man's mixed up in anything nasty. All sounds harmless enough, I know. But let me show you this'.

I must have been a good hour in the registrar's office that night, reading Dr Bruce's notes and listening to his rational interpretations. I was sceptical at first, but as his exposition continued became unable to suppress my admiration for the doctor's well conceived analyses.

There was nothing there to do with Poles, and the snag was that it was all convincing theory without anything that could be called proof. The Cold War had been filled with many false alarms of a similar nature. Out of two plus two it was all too easy for a lively mind to conjure six or seven. Though I did not blame the doctor. I thought it far more likely that Grant suffered from the common malady of needing to make himself seem important. A widower living alone. No family who cared enough about him to visit. All that was left to him was story-telling, something to hold the attention of someone at his bedside. Someone who paid him the compliment not just of listening but also of seeming to believe every word.

Young Dr Bruce thought that he was on to something, but before I accepted this I should need to hear something much more concrete.

I never saw the dying man again.

Grant talked to Dr Bruce once more next day. The doctor sent a porter to fetch me. The porter found my bed missing. It and I had been wheeled away for my neck to undergo a lengthy scan via nuclear magnetic resonance imaging.

Grant died while Dr Bruce was struggling to make sense of his final ramblings, and while I was in the scanner. That was that.

What more Dr Bruce might have learned, I had no way of knowing. My scan having proved satisfactory, it was decided to release me without operating to repair the break. I was delighted. To walk round for the rest of my life with a broken neck, that was going to be fun.

What did not occur to me was that if I had been kept in hospital for just one more day, I might have been given a much greater insight into the doings of the dying man and his two visitors. What more had Grant said to Dr Bruce in his last moments? In my joy at going home, I gave this question no thought.

I never again set eyes on Dr Bruce. Without any further details from him, all that I knew of possible Poles and 'something nasty' was that one man was dead, while a second wore steel-rimmed glasses and had the Christian name Bruce. Not very Polish-sounding. Once I was back home in Argyll, I forgot about the matter. Perhaps it had all been a fantasy on Dr Bruce's part.

Naturally, I was grateful to the man. From the moment that I was moved from the dying room into his care, the consulting neurosurgeon and he took total and unremitting care of me. What a contrast between their concern for my wellbeing and the 'let 'em thirst to death' policy in that corner room.

Unforgettable, too, were the nurses. Day or night, they gave me not just water, but coffee too, whenever I asked for it. It was these attentions, and the staff's otherwise incomparable care, that I recalled with such gratitude once I had been released. In the contented atmosphere of what had been my childhood home, memories of the Liverpool pathway faded into unthinkability.

Only one thing spoiled those first weeks back at home. I had still to wear a rigid, though comfortable, collar preventing any turning of the neck. This put the lid on any ideas I had about driving around on our tricky roads, where one needs eyes going from side to side like a pair of demented windscreen wipers. I ran up the motor of the E-Type from time to time, and, for the sake of the tyres, moved it to different positions along my drive.

The consulting neurosurgeon, Mr Hill-Forrester, still kept a particular eye on my progress. He was a handsome dark-haired man of around forty, distinguished in my eyes by a refusal to grasp easily at the first interpretation or solution presenting itself. I liked the way the man searched for every detail in his patients.

He called me back into hospital at regular intervals for x-rays and scans. A friend from the village, who had fetched my Jaguar home from outside Jardine's house, drove me to and from these appointments.

Mr Hill-Forrester waited a full six months after my silly fall before telling me: 'You can take your collar off'. I took more than that. I took the wheel of my friend's car for the journey back to Argyll.

Once indoors, my first job was cutting off, then shaving, six months' growth of beard. Next came a visit to the barber. To be home, to be collarless, to be fit to drive on all my errands without needing to enlist a friend – this was the highest level of bliss that I could expect without Anna.

Several times during my early days in hospital, when the hallucinatory drugs had worn off for the moment and I had some lucid thought back, I wished that I had followed Anna. I even cursed Jardine – may he forgive me – for pulling me back from death by seeing to it that my dehydration was ended.

It took a week or two before I realized how ungrateful of me were such sentiments. The doctors and nurses, too, had taken a deal of trouble over me – once I was on the ward. I had almost a duty, it seemed to me now, to live as long as possible out of thankfulness to them as well as to Jardine.

There was certainly no denying that I owed a further debt, to the young registrar whose remains had been found by horrified workmen just before daylight on the railway line near Helensburgh. It was to put an end to the villainy of the men who had killed Dr Bruce that I was standing there now in that black angle of the walls, waiting for them.

The rain had eased, and I was tempted to step forward to shake some of the water from my clothing. Couldn't chance it, though. No point letting myself be seen. Who knew when the men with the explosives would arrive, or who might be watching now?

IV

G HASTLY to think how all through those next months, while I was growing stronger every day, suffering nothing at all in my neck and generally enjoying life in my old family home, other people were collecting explosives and preparing to kill without compunction.

The words 'hospital registrar' at first meant nothing to me when they leaped out from a newspaper headline. 'Hospital registrar in rail death riddle'. Of course it was Dr Bruce. Dead on a line not far from Helensburgh. The newspaper reports seemed to indicate suicide. Suggested, at least, that the authorities were satisfied to call it suicide.

A young man with too much imagination. Or too much credulity. Had I been right about that? Or had the poor chap, whom I had liked very much, really stumbled onto something nasty, as he had thought? And if so, could that have any connection with his unpleasant death?

I doubted whether the likeable registrar had confided his suspicions to his consultant superior. Mr Hill-Forrester was a splendid man who never stopped taking trouble over his patients. For these, his concern seemed to be endless. Knowing the extent of the man's assiduity, I mistakenly saw it as a sign of fussing when he wrote making yet another appointment for x-rays only a few days after I had been examined once more and given an encouraging report.

Were things not as good as I had been told, after all? Well, the fracture had not worried me at the time. I was not going to let it bother me now.

There was only one word to describe the day of my appointment with the consultant. That word was a good old Scots one: dreich. From horizon to horizon, blackness. And a seemingly almost solid curtain of rain whichever way I pointed the E-Type.

I have always been a stickler for arriving at appointments punctually, and despite the weather was at the hospital in good time for this one. I went through the familiar routine of x-rays taken with my head at different angles, and Mr Hill-Forrester pronounced himself satisfied.

'Do you remember', he asked me, 'Doctor Bruce?'

'The registrar killed on the railway line? Yes, of course I do. I liked him very much'.

'So did I. What do you know about this horrible business?'

'Not a thing beyond what I read in the papers'.

'What did you read?'

'That the poor fellow appeared to have jumped in front of a train. No one seemed to know why'.

'You took it as suicide?'

'That's what the papers seemed to suggest'.

'Mr Greig, I knew the man very well. He would have been the last person in the world to commit suicide'.

The man had no difficulty at all in reading my scepticism. 'I know', he conceded. 'People always say that, don't they? And they are usually wrong, aren't they? Because nearly everyone can kill himself in the right circumstances. Or perhaps I should say in the wrong circumstances. I agree that no one can tell what is going on inside another person's mind. Shakespeare summed it up best: *There's no art to find the mind's construction in the face.* Yet in young Bruce's case there were clearly no circumstances of any kind that would have suggested suicide to him. He was about to be married, for pity's sake – and I never saw anyone quite so exhilarated at the prospect'.

The neurosurgeon raised a hand. 'I know, I know. There are such things as cold feet. But Dr Bruce did not have them, believe me. And if he had, why not just call the whole thing off? Why kill himself? In any case, like every doctor he had at his disposal a hundred comfortable means of killing himself. Jumping in front of a train would scarcely make any sense'.

'Unless he just decided on suicide on the spur of the moment, when he had no access to barbiturates'.

'But that's just what he did have. There were more than enough in a leather pouch that he carried with him in an inside pocket. There was a needle with two morphine ampoules as well. Smashed by the train, of course, but the police could see what he had on him'.

'And their conclusion was suicide? They ruled out accident?'

'It seemed far less likely to them that a fully grown man with no alcohol in him would wander inadvertently in front of a train, rather than that he should step in front of it deliberately. I have to say that statistics agree with them. Suicide on the railway is common enough. Accidents on the tracks are pretty rare'.

'Yet despite the fact that the man had the means to finish himself off more cleanly, you agree that he jumped in front of the train intentionally?'

'I didn't say that. I agreed that suicide was more likely than accident'.

'But all the same you believe that this was an accident?'

'I didn't say that, either'.

So that was where he was heading.

'You could see no motive for suicide', I reminded him. 'Can you see one for murder?'

'I can't, but I was rather hoping that you might be able to get to the bottom of the thing'.

Oh, he was, was he? I should have seen it coming. The man had quite the wrong impression of my abilities and experience. He reads my books, and assumes from them that I have superpowers and super connections. I needed to put him straight before this thing went any further.

'My books', I pointed out, 'are mainly fiction. Certainly they contain a series of real incidents that happened to me or to other people, but these are always attached to a basic fictional premise. You should not take the stories too seriously, and certainly not assume that I have any standing at all with the authorities. In any case, what makes you think Dr Bruce's death was neither suicide nor accident?'

'It was his briefcase'.

'His briefcase?'

'First, that he thought he needed such a case, and secondly, the fact that its contents had been taken'.

'Couldn't anyone coming across his body have emptied it? Particularly if he had drugs in it'.

'There were no drugs in the case'.

'How do you know?'

'Dr Bruce left his quarters to spend a weekend with his fiancée at her parents' home near Helensburgh. I was with him when he put papers into his case, and I drove him to the railway station. He took nothing besides a pile of papers, that I can swear'.

'Hospital papers?'

'We never take hospital papers off the premises. It is most strictly forbidden. In any case, I am certain that these were personal papers. I caught a glimpse of them, and can state most definitely that they bore not the least resemblance to the sort of records that we keep'.

'None of your papers missing?'

'Nothing at all'.

'Photocopiers in every department, I suppose?'

'Of course, but...'

'Dr Bruce would not have taken copies of anything?'

'Such a thing would have been entirely out of character, I assure you. Please – I am not defending the man simply because he was a colleague and a friend. I knew his character too well, and as I told you I glimpsed the papers that he took with him'.

'Any of them look as though they were in a foreign language at all? Polish, for instance?'

The surgeon looked puzzled. 'Polish? No. Why on earth...? Frankly, though, I didn't see the text at all'.

'It doesn't matter. It was just a thought. Those that you did see, that he definitely had with him, somebody took those. Whatever they were, they were of interest to someone else'.

'Yes. The case had been sliced apart by the train wheels and was empty'.

'Papers could have been blown away by the wind, couldn't they, once the case had been cut open?'

'Ah, but though it had been cut, the lid remained locked in place. It would have been necessary to slide the papers sideways out of the case. Human hand at work'.

'The police told you this, did they?'

'They showed me the case. They too wanted to know whether hospital papers could have been involved. There was the poor man's weekend bag, as well. That had been searched. Its contents had been strewn to the winds and its linings ripped out. Somebody was certainly looking for something'.

'And though he found whatever it was in the briefcase, this maybe wasn't enough, or he wouldn't have ripped the linings from the weekend bag as well'.

'Precisely. The police asked me the same questions as you. Were there hospital papers in the briefcase? Were any hospital papers missing?'

'If, as you believe, the papers were personal, have you any idea at all what they could have been to interest a thief?'

'Haven't the remotest clue'.

I had. A very positive clue. The notes that the young registrar had made of the dying Simon Grant's ramblings. Whoever took them from the briefcase could only be one of Grant's associates. He had killed for them.

'What were Dr Bruce's interests, his connections?'

'Outside his work and his fiancée, I should say that almost nothing else animated him'.

I had known one or two people like that, had been one myself. Did that make us dull dogs? Before Anna arrived, there was only my work. After she died, my work was again everything. Now, in premature retirement, I had no particular reason to rejoice that my fall had not finished me off. Except that it seemed as though something interesting might be cropping up right here.

'Did he have any Polish friends, do you know?'

'Polish?'

'Yes. Had he any, that you know of?'

'Never heard him speak of anyone Polish. But then, at university he could have met people from anywhere round the globe. Mind you, he wasn't the type to make many friends. His fiancée seemed to fill all his world outside the job'.

Poles. Plenty of them in Scotland, but who was to say that the ones who had upset the late Simon Grant had anything to do with Dr Bruce?

The briefcase was puzzle enough, without complications that might not be connected. The briefcase. Sliced open, yet not taken. Yes, it would have looked suspicious for anyone to carry a case in that condition. Better just to fold the papers and stuff them away in a pocket.

'Apart from the papers', I asked, 'had the body been robbed?'

'Not at all. He was still wearing his watch, his wallet was in his pocket and his pouch with medicines still where he always carried it. This helped to convince the police that it was suicide, certainly not a robbery murder'.

'Yet what did they make of the missing papers?'

'Very simple. They suggested that Dr Bruce must have passed them on to somebody en route'.

Hm. Couldn't deny that. All the same, I am always mistrustful of easy explanations. In this case, particularly since the briefcase in question had been chained to the doctor's wrist. Not much wrist left now, and the sliced up case had been lying loose. Didn't seem important to the police, apparently, but I couldn't help wondering why on earth a hospital registrar had felt the need for one of those wrist chain cases.

This was what Mr Hill-Forrester wondered, too.

Such cases were familiar enough in use by bank messengers, diamond merchants and the like. The Navy, too, had a purpose for them. Commanders of

Britain's nuclear submarines carried in such locked cases the numerical codes used in programming to their targets each of the 192 missiles carried on board their ships. These constituted Britain's massive strategic deterrent, the threat that it was hoped need never be used, that meanwhile preserved Britain's freedom from attack.

What could a junior hospital doctor need to carry and to protect in such an almost melodramatic fashion? Why had he felt it necessary to acquire such a secure item as a wrist chain case? What papers could have seemed so important to him that they had to be guarded so elaborately?

I had seen his notes on Grant's mutterings, and he could surely not have regarded those as of such significance. It must have been what the dying man said to him later, something that I had not heard, that convinced him of the need for top level precautions.

It was certainly impossible, if the doctor's death had been either accident or suicide, to explain the ransacking of both the briefcase and his weekend bag.

Grant's men, or 'those blasted Poles' who were their opponents? Who had known enough to retrieve his papers? And to murder him?

Murder. I had very nearly been charged with that myself, not so long ago – though I don't believe that the investigating detective had ever really been convinced I was guilty. That was in Berlin, not long after the Craigard trouble that had brought Jardine and myself together.

By this time, the Jardine baby, now in the South of England, was nearing his first birthday. During that first year of his life I had had plenty of opportunity to reflect on the thought that it was our surgeons who deserved the highest pay, not footballers or, heaven help us, 'pop' performers.

Nothing I could do about these matters, of course. It was time to concentrate on something where I could be of concrete help.

V

WHEN the door of the house at Helensburgh opened, I all but staggered under the shock. Anna! The same brown curly hair, the same wide set eyes, even the same dimples.

But of course it was not Anna. I had held Anna in my arms while she died. There could not be another, and nothing would ever deceive me that there were.

This was Dr Bruce's fiancée, Janine, and she looked as Anna had been in the early days of our marriage. Of course there were differences, and I saw these almost at once.

Very gently, I introduced myself as a former patient of the doctor, shocked to hear of his death. My tardiness in not appearing until so long afterwards I explained as due to my having only recently been discharged from the hospital where once the doctor had taken such good care of me.

A broken neck is a wonderful reason for not immediately rushing out and about, and I was invited into the house with the tenderest expressions of sympathy.

Janine's parents were an agreeable pair, younger than I expected and both noticeably slim. Her father, bright-eyed and vivacious, might even be considered bony. I was seated and on the point of accepting an offered cup of tea when the girl's father intervened with those most beautiful of all words: 'I'm sure you'll take something stronger, won't you?'

To my surprise, mother and daughter both joined in the taking of a dram.

'The best whisky', explained the girl's father, 'comes from bottles without labels'.

As if I needed to be told. Whisky that had come straight from the distillery or bonded warehouse without a penny in duty having being paid to HM Government had belonged to the very fabric of my growing up years.

'Let me guess', I asked. 'You work at a bottling plant'.

'As long as you're not a policeman. Or HM Revenue and Customs'.

I gave the requisite assurances, and we spoke about the dead man. Janine's parents had clearly admired and been fond of Dr Bruce. Having myself come to know him, though only superficially, I could understand this well enough. The late doctor had been the kind of man whose company one would always find delightful.

As for the girl, she became tearful almost from the start. 'Alasdair wouldn't have killed himself', she insisted. 'He wouldn't. I know he wouldn't'.

Inwardly, I agreed with her, but said nothing. Might it not be even more distressing, I wondered, to hear that someone had been murdered?

In any case, so far I had no proof of anything. Only an inner conviction.

'They wouldn't even let me see him', Janine complained.

Her mother's hand closed softly over the girl's. 'Darling, he was very badly injured indeed. It is better that you keep the memories you have'.

'So you keep telling me'.

I managed to turn thoughts to the practical by asking whether Dr Bruce had left a key with Janine.

'His key? Yes'.

'May I see it?'

Apparently the police had not asked about a key. I was anxious to try it in the lock to the wrist chain.

Janine agreed to let me take the key, provided that I returned it. It was a memento of her fiancé that she wished to retain.

I asked about papers, and was met with blankness. No, Dr Bruce had never left any papers at his intended's home. Nor, apparently, had he done any paperwork there.

Had the doctor spoken at all of Poles during the last weeks of his life?

Poles? No. Never mentioned any.

I drove from Helensburgh to see the doctor's parents. These were a different proposition, dour and evangelistically teetotal. In contrast to Janine's parents, Dr. Bruces' father and mother were both pleasantly rounded in body. Though polite and friendly enough, the couple struck me as probably belonging to one of those smaller churches known for their strictness and austerity. Stereotypes were being destroyed here, I thought. One might have expected the cheerful couple to be plump, the sternly religious to be meagre in body.

Dr Bruce's charm had clearly been self-developed, not inherited. To his parents, suicide was unthinkable. I had the impression that religious dogma was behind this attitude. They had made up their minds that their son had fallen victim to a ghastly accident. How this had happened they did not attempt to explain even to themselves, but remained content in the nebulous refuge of 'accident'.

Despite the Bruces' coldness there was no point in my being diffident. I asked straight out to examine their son's room, and they acquiesced without demur. Doubtless they hoped that I should find something to destroy the suicide theory once and for all.

I didn't. I found medical books, medical papers. The relics of six years at university. Letters from Janine, parcelled up and stowed at the back of a cupboard. Mr Hill-Forrester was right. Outside his work and his fiancée, Dr Bruce appeared to have had no interests.

I searched for papers hidden inside others. I hunted through desk, cupboards and wardrobe, explored under the doctor's bed.

Nothing. No documents – that is, none outside medical and personal notes.

A box of personal possessions, packed up and returned to his parental home from staff accommodation at the hospital, also yielded nothing. And no sign of the notes that the doctor had shown to me that night in the hospital, those he had compiled from what a dying patient imagined to be his confidences. This seemed to confirm that these were what he had carried with him in his briefcase, the papers that his killer had sought and taken.

One minor item attracted my attention, not because it had any significance, but because it aroused my curiosity. On the envelope of a letter to the doctor, dated two days before he died, the words *'Going It Alone'* had been written in ink, crossed out and replaced with *'The Lion's Mouth'*. What struck me was that each of these words was capitalized, suggesting that they represented titles of something or other – perhaps of songs. The words meant nothing to me at the time. After checking that the handwriting matched other examples of the doctor's script, I forgot about the matter.

There was no computer and no printer. No, father and mother assured me, they had never seen any computer. Their son had written everything laboriously by hand. There was, though, a key to match the one I had been given by Janine. I took it with me.

I asked about possible Polish contacts, and again met with blankness.

On the drive home I began to wonder about silly things. A railway locomotive – was that a blunt instrument? The largest one could use, perhaps, except for an aircraft. It would be fascinating to see a skilled pilot fly into someone on the ground and gain height again. How about flying into a parachutist? But how could I forget a ship? Squash someone into the wall of a harbour, or run him down in the water. Anyway, could a locomotive's wheels be regarded as blunt?

I was torn from such nonsense by the realization that the car in my rear view mirror was a 'tail'. Whether it was the accumulated experience of years, or simple instinct, I cannot say. Whatever the explanation, I knew beyond doubt that the man behind me was following with a fixed purpose. Not a police effort, though. I doubted whether police had manpower to spare for that sort of thing. They could have alerted my old Service to my unauthorized inquiries, and done no more than that. I could not believe, though, that in the car behind me was someone sent by my former colleagues. Certainly not anyone I had trained. Otherwise I should never have been able to spot him.

One of 'those blasted Poles', perhaps?

I decided to have some fun.

In what part of the country my tail was used to driving, I had no idea. I, though, had grown up on Highland roads, and knew exactly where I could dive into off-road cover.

An E-Type is just about the most recognizable car on the roads. Despite this, I was able to conceal its shape by whipping round behind whins within three seconds of leaving the carriageway. I watched my tail sail past, and popped out after him. I was actually able to see the man jump in his seat when in his mirror he spotted me behind him.

Five miles farther on, I stopped in a village with an Italian-owned shop, bought an ice cream and leaned on my car to enjoy it. I rarely had an ice without remembering my paternal grandfather, who had deceived my infant self with his fairy tale that ice cream was in reality elephant's eggs. When I told Anna about this, she laughed, commented: 'I should like to have met your grandfather', and added: 'When we have children, we shall tell them the same story, and wait to see how long it takes them to discover the truth'.

Of course, we never did have any children. Anna was rather hoping that it would happen, when the KGB cut her life short. I suppose I should not complain too much, considering the damage that Anna herself had apparently done to the Soviet Union. Even so, Anna's death was an unpleasant one, and I still find it difficult to think of her as just another casualty of the Cold War.

Ice cream demolished, I ambled homewards at a pace that the men from Jaguar Cars would have considered a disgrace. Their creation was never built to crawl, and could scarcely function efficiently at very low revs.

A mile or two along the road, there was my tail. Parked in a passing place, which he had evidently mistaken for a lay-by. This was a common error among Sassenachs and others unfamiliar with roads outside the Central Belt.

I slid up alongside. The man sat staring into a road map that he held high in a defensive V shape.

That he was clearly determined neither to turn his head nor to acknowledge my arrival would alone have told me that he was untrained. The first thing that I hammered into all my protégés was the necessity of behaving with complete naturalness.

I appeared at his side window and tapped. The face that turned to me was remarkable for a large curved nose. Not a fat nose, nor a nose with a bump, but a slim clean curve suggestive of a neatly cut quadrant.

A Polish nose? Silly idea. A neb like that could belong to any race.

'Do you know that this is not a lay-by?' I asked. 'It is a passing place. It is needed both for overtaking and for allowing a vehicle to come by from the opposite direction. You can't park here without causing obstruction to legitimate traffic'.

I admit that I was exaggerating. While what I had said was true of passing places on Highland roads in general, the carriageway here was wider than the average, and my tail's parking was unlikely to obstruct many vehicles.

'Oh, I'm sorry. I didn't know'. An agitated hand groped for the ignition key. The map crumpled.

I looked towards the creased and wrinkled paper. 'Did you manage to work out where you are going?'

'Oh yes. Yes, thank you'.

I forbore to suggest that he follow me, though I was tempted.

The man's voice was Scots. Meaningless, of course. Grow up in Scotland, and you'll speak with a Scots accent, no matter what the nationality of your parents. Even so – a sinister Pole? I all but laughed at myself for burgeoning paranoia.

I couldn't know then what evil the man with the remarkable nose had in his armoury.

After that, I streaked away from my supposed shadow, whoever he was, putting my foot down through all the twistiest sections of road. No doubt the man was still wondering where the hell I had gone when I was already sitting in my lounge with the E-Type locked behind garage doors.

VI

Owls I had always believed to have wonderful night vision. Whether this is true or otherwise, I assume that owls can make mistakes like the rest of us. As I stood waiting in the deep shadow of my corner, an owl swooped practically into my face, spotted me only at the last second and swerved flapping away. Not a large owl, but an owl. Perhaps I was standing where the bird sometimes perched. If so, I must have annoyed him greatly. Probably, too, he had been as startled as I was.

An owl, I thought, was a rarity in the heart of the city. Yet what did I know? I could be as wrong about birds as I had been about Dr Bruce. No interests outside his work and his fiancée, Mr Hill-Forrester had said, and I had accepted this.

Enlightenment came in a large, heavy letter. Not, though, one addressed to me.

A telephone call from Mr Hill-Forrester's secretary invited me for the next afternoon. The neurosurgeon received me in his consulting room as soon as I arrived, unlocked a cupboard, reached in and handed me a postal packet.

The envelope was of something more than A4 size, perhaps an inch and a half thick, and heavy. It was addressed to Dr Bruce at the hospital. The address label bore the name of an Edinburgh publishing house of which I had never heard.

'Arrived yesterday morning', Mr Hill-Forrester explained. 'Strictly speaking, I should send everything on to his parents, and I shall do. I just thought that you might want to see this first'.

I slit open the package. Well bound in a heavy duty plastic folder, a typescript slid out into my hands. Clipped to it was a letter regretting that the enclosed story was too short for the publishing house's list. A novel, the letter writer pointed out, should contain ideally 80,000 to 85,000 words, whereas Dr Bruce's work had fewer than 30,000.

I put the letter into Mr Hill-Forrester's hands. Once he had read it, I opened the typescript so that we could examine this together. *Going It Alone* was the title. I now knew the meaning of the note that Dr Bruce had written out for himself. He had thought of a better title: *The Lion's Mouth.* This had been written on a letter dated only two days before his death, so clearly represented the author's final intention. OK. *The Lion's Mouth* it should be.

Why, Mr Hill-Forrester wondered aloud, had Dr Bruce submitted the work from his hospital address.

It did not surprise me. Having met his parents, I could imagine that it would be impossible for him to keep anything private at home. If I were engaged on a first literary venture, but living with dry-as-dust family at home, I should certainly have been inclined to keep it to myself. The doctor must have written and printed his work at the hospital, presumably during standby hours at night. Did the police have any knowledge of his effort? I doubted it.

I offered to leave the typescript with Mr Hill-Forrester, for him to read first. He shook his head. 'Good lord! Enjoyed your books, that poor old Bruce lent me, but so short staffed these days, hardly find time to read the latest issue of the *British Medical Journal*. I'd never wade through that lot. You take it away, and you can let me know if there's anything in it that you think significant'.

Dr Bruce's story was a fantasy. When writers imagine what the future will be like, we call their tales 'futuristic'. What do we call a fanciful re-imagining of the past? I knew that people had written stories showing how they imagined the world would have become if something or other had happened that never did happen. Never, though, heard any label for that sort of work.

The event Dr Bruce had pictured was that Scotland achieved independence in the early 1930s. How, he speculated, would a Scottish government, self-centred and determined to follow a path distinct from that of England and Wales, have dealt with the international events that were to come? Not the best story I've ever read, I must say. On the other hand, not worth killing the author, I shouldn't have thought. Unless one were a particularly severe and intolerant literary critic.

One would need to be blind not to recognize the parallels that the doctor drew with today's situation. Nationalists of the past hoping to profit from Scotland's production of whisky; those in the present looking to a bonanza from North Sea oil.

I must say that I am far from certain whether the doctor had chosen the right format for his work. The narrative of an imagined alternative past remains unconvincing for people who know what really did happen and are proud of their successful part in it.

Much more persuasive would surely have been a future fantasy in which Scotland becomes independent a few years hence, runs quickly into serious financial difficulties and is soon turning to England and Wales for help.

Of course, I may be wrong.

Whatever the work's merits or lack of them, as an intended warning to the nation, the late doctor's effort at least possesses a certain degree of intellectual content.

If you take the trouble to read Dr Bruce's work, you will be able to decide for yourself. Are his ideas too fanciful? Or all too realistic? Either way, they surely suggest no reason to push the author under a train.

No obligation to read through the thing, of course. You can simply skip forward to chapter seven, if you prefer. Or chuck this whole book into the paper recycling bin. I believe, though, that Dr Bruce's ideas are worth a thought and that he deserves a reading.

See what you think.

The Lion's Mouth
1

JUST when you thought it was safe to go back into...
being a separate nation again.

I never had much time for politics. Finding myself looking into the muzzle of a German submachine gun, that was what woke me up. That, and having seen at close range a group of my fellow countrymen lined up against a wall and shot.

Believe me, when one finds the business end of a firearm pointing close up directly into one's face, the barrel appears suddenly to be of enormous diameter.

That black hole had a way of holding my attention.

The German, on the other hand, was looking at me with what I thought was less purpose than the situation demanded. That was what it looked like, and if I was right it would mean that he was letting his concentration slip.

I measured the distance between us. Barely five feet. I made a rapid downward swoop with my right hand.

The German was just as quick. In the instant that my fingers hit the hilt of my sgian dubh, a metallic klunk came from his submachine gun. It was the sound of a heavy bolt striking a firing chamber, and it was something that I should not have been able to hear. When the bolt of a submachine gun reaches the forward limit of its travel, it is supposed to pierce the percussion cap of the round that is in the chamber, and so begin a burst of continuous fire.

One of two things had saved my life. Either the firing pin – a projection on the bolt – was damaged, or the round in the SMG's chamber had a dud percussion cap. Such a thing does happen. Of the many millions turned out during wartime, the odd ineffective round will always slip through into the mountains of supplies that go forward to the troops. Whichever was the cause of this misfire, the question mattered less than whether I or the German would react faster.

I froze for an instant before drawing my sgian dubh. The German froze for a little longer. My blade was through his throat almost before I was aware of putting it there. The German's eyes widened, his mouth worked. His body had not sagged to the ground before I was reaching for the SMG that had slipped there ahead of him. I had the top round out of the weapon before wiping the German's blood from my sgian dubh. The percussion cap showed the proper indentation, so it had been hit correctly. A single tiny flaw, undetectable until too late. It had cost the German his life, and saved mine.

There was no damage to the firing pin. The weapon was fine, and thirty-one rounds were left in the magazine. Good. I should make effective use of these.

It had been only five days since the German invasion, yet I felt as though I had been on the move for a month without a firearm. Thank goodness for my sgian dubh.

The snag was that the Germans were liable to take the first ten villagers on whom they could lay their hands and shoot them like the men I had already seen shot. The only way to avoid this would be for me to go to the Germans and confess.

The whole situation should never have happened. Scotland ought never to have been invaded.

If only we had stuck with the English...

Independence, they had called it, but how independent were we now?

Germans in Edinburgh, issuing decrees. Germans along the Clyde, shooting skilled shipyard men who refused to work for them. Germans all through our farming country, helping themselves to the bulk of the meat and to everything else. Germans outside our fishing ports, sinking any vessel on a course they thought suspicious.

Surely we should have seen it coming.

At the time of separation from the UK, I had been too young to vote. In any case, I had my head full of other things. Foolishly, I believed that the men in Parliament, spending all their time with these issues, knew what was best for us and could safely be left to do what was right.

In any case, the people had voted for separation, hadn't they? I had myself been against the idea, but if a majority of my countrymen thought that it was desirable, what did any dissenting view matter?

It was the voice of the majority that counted.

This was what we believed in, this is what we thought fair. Wise? Well, I never heard anyone claim that; but fair, anyway. No, political questions had not caught my attention while I was growing up. I could not argue from any position of particular knowledge. My opposition to separation from the UK had been a matter of instinctive feeling, nothing more.

Do your job, whatever it might be, to the best of your ability, all the time – that was what I believed was the right thing to do. If everyone did that, then nothing much bad could happen to the country.

Sadly, this assumption did not allow for political extremism. When I heard the word nationalism, it meant, I thought, pride in one's country. I did not realize then that it meant placing one's own interests above those of other nations and above the common interests of all peoples.

Of course, everyone knew that there was to be No More War. We knew it, the French knew it, and the Germans knew it. Few slogans – perhaps none – found more universal resonance. All history had taught us, nonetheless, that an unforeseen troublemaker was likely to pop up at any moment. We should therefore remain fully armed at all times, just in case.

I always knew that I should follow my father into his regiment, as he had followed his. There was no question of my choosing any other career. With luck, Britain would never need to be defended. Yet only a fool relies on luck. And even were Britain herself not threatened, her interests overseas might come under attack. In such an eventuality, I wanted to be there, to do my bit for my people.

My father had been killed during the last year of the War to End Wars. At the end of 1918, Mother and I moved out of the officers' married quarters at Fort George, near Inverness, and into a house just outside Oban. Here we were close to my paternal grandparents, who never ceased to encourage me in my two dominating interests: my love of Scotland and my desire to bear arms in her service.

From my grandmother I learned much of the poetry of Sir Walter Scott, from my grandfather the details of past battles by which great issues had been decided.

'Now that we have made the world safe for democracy', the old man told me, making no attempt to suppress the scepticism in his voice, 'we are supposed to settle these matters by discussion. There'll be no more going for the other fellow's throat; just talking to him through the League of Nations',

I had been away at school in Edinburgh for six years before I was old enough to enter the Royal Military College at Sandhurst. That was the same year that economic misery began spreading across the world after the Stock Market crash. By the time I passed out from Sandhurst, things had become even worse. Banks had apparently collapsed, though how a bank could collapse was beyond me. Surely, banks held all the country's money.

As you can see, I knew nothing of the world in those days. My head was filled solely with all those matters that command a freshly gazetted second lieutenant's attention.

2

IT took a visit to Glasgow with a regimental comrade to wake me to what those headlines about 'depression' and 'crisis' meant to my fellow countrymen.

I had never before seen, or even imagined, groups of working men – now not-working men – standing around or leaning at street corners, apathetic, faces grey, demeanour exhibiting an unmistakable absence of hope. I saw them now, at Yarrow and past mile after mile of shipyards and docks, once full of clang and clash, now fallen dormant.

I saw their womenfolk, too – or some of them – haggard and shabby, in their hands shopping bags that were all but empty, trudging the streets with heads down, miserably oblivious to the sunshine of a glorious August day.

Later, I learned that unemployment in Glasgow had reached thirty per cent of working age men. This, I believe, was the highest proportion to be found anywhere in Britain.

Into the poverty and the desperation fresh voices now spoke up. People had heard the Communists and their violent notions for a panacea. Had heard and in their sensible majority had ceased to listen. They had heard the less radical Socialists, and found these not just acceptable, but promising. Most had reposed their hopes there, and found that after all the Socialists brought them nothing. The second Labour government in six years produced no amelioration in their hardships.

The fresh sound that now came to the Scottish people in their despair had a seductive tone. It promised a way out of their poverty and had an attractive simplicity. It was also flattering, and who is not susceptible to a little praise?

'The best people to govern Scotland' it urged, 'are those who live here, not others down at Westminster'.

Scots the best people to govern Scotland? Sounded good. During the war, control over domestic affairs by the Westminster government had of necessity been tightened and extended. That, argued the seducers, was English imperialism. We had to throw it off.

No thought was given to the economic and defensive strength that union had given us.

Before the war there had been much talk, and some expectation, of home rule for Scotland. And why not? people now asked. Ireland had it. At least, those parts of Ireland that wanted it. All at once, the notion of self-determination ceased to appear an impossible dream. A vision of Scottish independence lit a beacon of expectation.

Away from Westminster! Away from constant subservience to English requirements! Pre-war, Scottish home rule had been a central policy within the Labour movement. The Labour Party still paid lip service to the idea, but when in power at

Westminster declined to allow any debate, let alone a division, on a home rule bill. It could be no surprise when the privations caused by the general economic crash caused Scottish support for the Labour government to collapse. Labour had let them down. That was the central point on which most were agreed.

Into the void stepped the National Party of Scotland. Its declared aim: the establishment of a free 'Socialistic Commonwealth of Scotland'.

The socialism was fundamental. NPS members were not National Socialists, but they were Social Nationalists. And they did share the National Socialist characteristics of intolerance, even contempt, towards those who would not be convinced by them, along with a ruthless determination to impose their aims and values on their whole people.

NPS members now buckled down to the task of preparing a campaigning machine for fighting the next election, whenever that might come.

It came in October 1931. The NPS put up candidates in every constituency in Scotland.

The party had a landslide victory. Of seventy four MPs sent to Westminster by voters in Scotland, fifty seven were Nationalists. Even ignoring the much castigated 'first-past-the-post' electoral system, a count of total votes cast showed that the NPS would have had a similarly convincing win under the proportional representation arrangement. Now the weak Westminster government found itself in no position to oppose NPS demands for independence.

The Labour leader Ramsay MacDonald (a Scotsman from Lossiemouth) was propped up in power only by Conservatives and some Liberals. Even many of his own party opposed him, refusing to be part of a coalition government.

The best resistance that Westminster could offer to demands for independence was to hold out – on Conservative insistence – for a referendum on the issue. Unsurprisingly, and with some justification, the NPS claimed that its successes in the October election had already amounted to a referendum, with a clear majority for independence. Why did they need to go through it again?

In the end, NPS leaders gave in. What had they to lose from a referendum? A result in their favour was already certain. Sadly for the peoples of these islands, they were right.

March 24, 1932, was the day of decision in Scotland. Seventy one point eight per cent of those who voted gave a clear 'yes' to the question 'Do you want Scotland to leave the United Kingdom and forthwith administer its own affairs as an independent sovereign country in its own right?'

I myself was still too young to vote, but had I been old enough should certainly have given my 'No!'

Westminster had insisted that a simple majority would not be enough. Before independence could be granted, two thirds of Scots voters must agree. This threshold having been comfortably exceeded, the NPS pressed for June 24, 1932, as the date for Scotland to secede from the Union to which she had adhered for two hundred and twenty five years. June 24 was favoured because it was the date, in 1314, of the Battle of Bannockburn. Another candidate in the calendar was April 6. On that day in 1320 the Declaration of Arbroath had been sent to the Pope, asserting Scottish independence as a sovereign state.

Finally, after much wrangling, secession was set for Friday, July 1, 1932. Nationalists now looked forward to what they believed would be the third great date in their nation's history.

NPS leaders quickly lost themselves in arguments about the design of a new national coat of arms, the pattern for a Scottish passport and jobs for the laddies – most of all the choice of ambassadors whom they would despatch to the world's governments.

First, the composition of Scotland's Parliament had to be decided. In an adaptation of the American pattern, an upper house was to be created with one senator from each county. The election for the Edinburgh Parliament, held on June 16, returned a sound majority for the NPS in both houses, with the Labour Party well behind in second place.

Two Liberal members and a lone Conservative would complete the composition of the lower house, with just one Liberal in the Senate.

Now, triumphed the Nationalists. Scottish brains, Scottish enterprise and Scottish hard work would see to it that unemployment was cut to a minimum and that those unfortunate few for whom work was not immediately found would be given adequate benefits. And we should always earn a lot from our exports of whisky. Plus – and this point was stressed ad infinitum – tax from whisky would now go to the Scottish Government for the benefit of the Scottish people, not to Westminster to be frittered away on Scotland's neighbours.

3

OFFICIALLY, Scotland became independent at one minute past midnight on Friday, July 1, 1932. The moment was marked with firework displays in nearly every city and town across the land. The biggest display, centred on the castle, was at Edinburgh, where the formal opening of Scotland's new parliament took place at 11am.

Eager to demonstrate *de facto* Scotland's new *de jure* position as an independent sovereign state, her leaders despatched their first ambassador that same morning – to the Court of St James. The English took their time with reciprocation. It was not until ten days later that an English ambassador arrived in Edinburgh.

The most sought-after ambassadorial post within Scotland's new Ministry of Foreign Affairs was the appointment to Washington. Only moderately less coveted was accreditation to Moscow. Among the radical Socialists and covert Communists who had swollen the numbers of the NPS were many eager to experience the Soviet paradise at first hand. They had read the books, they had fantasized the dream. One day, they would be instrumental in the foundation of the Soviet Socialist Republic of Scotland. Until then, they could only study the ideal created by Moscow, study and learn, study and admire, study and envy.

Effectively, the Scots had a Socialist government, and were content with this. How strongly the extreme left-wing element featured within the NPS was unclear to the majority of Scotland's people.

First measures to put the unemployed back into work included a government contract for an ocean liner to be built on Clydeside. This was a purely speculative scheme, the government gambling on finding a purchaser. While the worldwide slump continued, none of the great shipping lines was likely to be adding to its fleet, or even replacing its ageing vessels. Ships that had long since amortized their costs would be required to keep on sailing for another year or two. Nonetheless, the hope was that by the time the

Clydeside liner was completed, the depression would have ended.

Meanwhile, the Edinburgh Parliament's sole Conservative member urged that, alongside the work on a civilian passenger ship, life could be put back into Clydeside with orders for one or more warships. This was roundly rejected by the House, an aggressive pacifist from the NPS condemning the suggestion as 'an obscenity'.

Pacifism was at the core of both NPS and Labour beliefs. The two controlling parties refused to prepare for a war that they were convinced would not happen. Even if, against all reasoned expectation, a war should break out somewhere, Scotland would remain aloof from it.

An aspect of Scotland's secession from the UK that attracted little notice at the time was in the division of Britain's armed forces. Scotland retained all specifically Scottish cavalry and infantry regiments, except for the Scots Guards, plus a single regiment of artillery. It was by express wish of His Majesty King George V, now sovereign of the United Kingdom of England, Wales and Northern Ireland, that the Scots Guards remained part of the English Army. A wholehearted welcome would be given, so London guaranteed, to any Scot who wished to serve in this historic regiment.

A token Scottish Air Force was established – to many, it seemed, unwillingly – with the acceptance from the RAF of a single squadron of Bristol Bulldog fighters. These were based at Turnhouse, on the outskirts of Edinburgh.

A destroyer and two frigates were all that NPS leaders considered necessary to protect any possible threat to Scotland's shores and sea lanes. It was said that England's Sea Lords partied well into the night in delight after what seemed to them inexplicably inadequate demands from Edinburgh.

Personnel transfer was voluntary. Scots servicemen who wished to remain in the English forces were allowed to do so. Few chose this option. In the main, Scotsmen proved eager to serve with their own country's military. I too remained with my regiment, despite grave reservations about the course that my misguided countrymen had chosen.

In those years after the wholesale slaughter of 1914-18, 'No More War' was an understandable fervent hope, if not a realistic expectation. For the NPS, 'no more war' was an article of faith. Holding defence to be a superfluous consideration, its unconcerned leaders were determined to maintain only the barest minimum of forces.

The proposal to revive warship construction on the Clyde was raised and rejected as the first item of business in the Edinburgh Lower House shortly after 10am on a Monday morning.

Next day I read that at almost the exact moment that this idea was voted down (shortly after 11am in Berlin), Germany's President von Hindenburg had named Adolf Hitler as the country's new Chancellor.

4

I MANAGED to put the foregoing together, you understand, only after a little research. At the time, all those intricacies of traffic between this group, that group and some other group might have been taking place in Outer Mongolia for all that I was aware of them. I took in that the people were being asked to break out of the United Kingdom, and that was all.

The notion appalled me. As far as I could see, the Act of Union had been one of the greatest political triumphs in history – indeed, one of history's very few unqualified successes. Together, we were always able to stand up to the rest of the world. As an amalgamated unit, since 1707 we British had fought off the French, the French again (this time when they were aided by the Spanish), the Dutch, the French yet once more and latterly, for the first time, the Germans. We had done damned well together, and I questioned whether we should do as well apart from each other. Only those who really believed that there would be No More War, I thought, could commit such folly.

Besides, the idea of a frontier, complete with barriers and Customs posts, stretching between Carlisle and Berwick appeared to me to be just plain silly. A retrograde step, if ever there were one.

Not that anybody asked me. As I have said, I was not of age to vote, and if I had been my 'No' would have meant nothing.

Horrified though I was at the break-up of the UK, I could scarcely criticize an industrious people plunged into sudden and undeserved poverty for clutching at the straw held out by the NPS. They could justifiably claim that no party at Westminster had helped them in their misery. What had they to lose, then, by giving someone else a chance? I could not blame the electorate, but I could and did blame the seducers.

I defer to no man or woman in my love for Scotland. You may take the intense depth of that love for granted.

From boyhood I had always thought of myself as Scots first and British second.

The catastrophic experience of supposed independence has since made me realize that I had been seeing things the wrong way round. Surely, we all of us in these islands are British first, and only then Scots, English, Welsh or Northern Irish.

The NPS played on every emotional and sentimental element in the people's psyche. The Scots were right, are right and always will be right to take pride in their history, their achievements and their abilities. Exploiting this pride perhaps brought the NPS more new supporters than any reasoned argument could have done. Sentiment, though, was never a sound basis for the gravest life-determining decisions. The misled electorate had cooperated with the NPS in its own seduction. We were to find out where over-nationalistic delusion was to lead.

So too were the German people, whose votes had made Hitler's party the largest single faction in the Reichstag.

Once in power, Hitler lost no time in recalling Germany's freshly appointed ambassador in Edinburgh and replacing him with one of the Nazi Party's faithful. On his appointment, the new man brought with him a personal letter from Hitler to Nicholas MacKerrel, leader of both the NPS and the Edinburgh Government. The German Chancellor congratulated MacKerrel on leading the Scots people to 'the freedom that would allow them to fulfil their natural destiny'. He gave his assurance that Germans wished to live in peace with the Scottish people, whose great qualities he personally had come to learn and to respect during the Great War.

This last was just the sort of thing that NPS leaders loved to hear. It was true that in his book *Mein Kampf* Hitler had made complimentary mention of the qualities of Scots soldiers.

For Scotland's far left, though, nothing that Hitler did or said could expiate his unpardonable anti-Communism. This became an issue in 1936, when several hundred volunteers set out from Scotland for Spain to fight with the International Brigade in the newly broken out Civil War. On the other side in this conflict, General Francisco Franco's forces were receiving reinforcements from Germany and Italy.

To support the Republican cause, for which the International Brigade fought, supplies of tanks arrived from the Soviet Union.

These, though, were despatched by Stalin not out of comradely solidarity. All Soviet deliveries had to be paid for in gold.

While the issue in Spain was being decided, Hitler occupied the Czech state, leaving Slovakia, nominally independent, to be ruled by a German puppet.

Fearing that Poland might be Hitler's next victim, England and France issued a guarantee to Warsaw that they would protect Polish borders.

We now know what had been top secret at the time, namely, that London made determined efforts to persuade the Edinburgh Government to join in the Polish guarantee.

Pacifism being a fundamental tenet of NPS attitudes, all such efforts were doomed from the outset to be fruitless.

Should Hitler attack Poland, England and France would come to her aid. Scotland would stand aside in self-satisfied neutrality. While our nearest neighbours engaged in vital combat against a wicked and rapacious régime, we were to remain lookers-on. A fine piece of conduct of which to be proud!

Soldiers, though, do not decide for themselves where and when they fight. They are servants of the state and carry out the policies of their governments. When they are told to remain in their barracks and do nothing, then that is what they do. No state could function in any other way.

The Spanish Civil War ended in mid-1939 with the victory of Franco's forces. Scottish survivors from the International Brigade – Communists, trade unionists and others – returned home filled with bitterness. The intervention of German forces had, they felt, been the deciding factor in the defeat of the Republican cause.

In a matter of weeks the rancour of these 'idealists', who had fought to ensure a Stalin-type dictatorship in Spain, turned to stupefaction. Their Communist idol and master signed a pact with Hitler.

5

NOW the world's Communists did not know where they were. This is how it is when people surrender their minds to an ideology. They need to wait to be told how they feel about every single issue.

I find it astonishing that so many people simply do not realize how precious are their minds. It is these alone that create our identity, that make us individuals. Physically, we all function in precisely the same way. Being able to reason is the one activity that each of us can pursue in his or her own unique fashion.

We do not have to behave like a flock of sheep, all going in exactly the same direction and at just the same pace. We, alone among the creatures of this world, can each work out even abstract concepts for ourselves. So why on earth would anyone surrender his or her distinctive and most treasurable possession to the dictates of a fellow being? From the moment of this renunciation, one is intellectually dead. Adherence to an ideology effectively ends one's existence as an individual. One might as well shuffle right off this mortal coil at once, and be done with it.

For decades now we have seen Communists degrading themselves to the level of sheep. And voluntarily! That is the inexplicable thing. More recently, we have watched the German people, too, submitting to the dictates of an ideology whose purpose defies understanding by the free, healthy mind. Even so, regimented as they are, I don't doubt that there were Germans, too, who wondered why their Führer, after ranting for so long against the evils of Communism, had now allied himself with the High Priest of that creed.

Certainly Communists everywhere were knocked completely off balance by the Hitler-Stalin pact. There was no point asking them their views on what had happened. True to their voluntary mindlessness, they had first to wait for Moscow to tell them what they were to think and what they were to say. Meanwhile, the only refuge of the Marxist faithful was to avoid discussion.

A week after the conclusion of the extraordinary German-Soviet pact, Hitler's forces did just what all who were not blind expected them to do. They invaded Poland. This left the governments of England and France with no alternative.

They declared war on Germany.

In Edinburgh, the German Ambassador was summoned to Holyrood to receive the Scottish Government's assurance that

Scotland would remain neutral throughout anything that might follow.

A fortnight later, with Poland on her knees, Soviet forces entered the stricken country from the east.

At Fort George, we devoured every newspaper on the market. The English titles had preference over our Scottish dailies, since their war reports tended to be more up to date and exhaustive. In the mess, we passed each issue from hand to hand, soaked up every report as though we were ourselves on our way to join the fight and needed to be briefed on every detail. We cut out situation maps and pinned these on our notice board. When news broadcasts were due, particularly the English ones, we gathered round the wireless set in a body. I had never known such silence in our mess. We listened as if we were to take an examination afterwards and needed to commit each word to memory. We went into Inverness to visit the cinema, solely in order to watch the newsreels.

The measure of our excitement was matched only by the level of our frustration.

All was over very quickly. Regrettably, neither England nor France was able to intervene in Poland. Polish territory was divided between the two powerful dictatorships.

Hitler had settled his issue with the Poles – that of territory taken from Germany in 1919. So far as England and France were concerned, that did not end hostilities. The French, reinforced by an English Expeditionary Force, lay in wait behind their strong eastern defences, ready at any moment to fight off a German invasion. Now not just we at Fort George, but the whole world waited to see when Hitler would strike in the west.

Instead, he went north. Denmark and Norway were occupied in lightning strokes. English and French forces landed in Norway, but were unable to dislodge the Germans.

During the struggle to save Norway, England's Premier Chamberlain made a personal appeal to Scotland's head of government, Nicholas MacKerrel, asking for the use of Scottish harbours for Royal Navy ships. This would have involved Scapa Flow in the Orkneys, and on the east coast Aberdeen, Montrose and probably Rosyth, too. MacKerrel rejected this plea out of hand. Nothing was to compromise Scotland's declared and sacrosanct neutrality.

The English responded at once to Hitler's western assault, when it came, by mobilizing their own super-weapon. Winston Churchill became Prime Minister on the same day that German forces crossed into France.

It became quickly apparent how valuable Churchill was to become during the dangerous times ahead.

Hitler's victory over France was breathtaking in its tempo. As soldiers we could only follow each news broadcast in astonishment and, gradually, with grudging professional admiration. The effect of Germany's western offensive was to draw many Scots to join England's forces. Some had already headed south at the outbreak of hostilities, and those first volunteers had been simply absorbed into existing regiments, air force squadrons or the crews of warships.

The new influx from Scotland now so eclipsed the early arrivals in number that it was possible to raise within the English Army two specific brigades of Scots – 'this hardy, well-proven and indomitable people', as Churchill called us in one of his unforgettable broadcast speeches.

The incongruity, absurdity – and shame – of Scotland's position was well illustrated during Operation Dynamo,

England's rescue of her soldiers (and many French ones) from Dunkirk and other points along France's northern coast. A Scottish coaster, the Capercaillie, had just unloaded her cargo at Tilbury when the call came for every available vessel to set off for the Dunkirk beaches.

Capercaillie's master, Alexander Wilson McKenzie, at once abandoned the loading of the return freight that he was to carry to Leith, and set off at full engine speed for France. Capercaillie brought back to safety 127 men of the English Expeditionary Force who were being machine-gunned from the air on a French beach.

Despite damage sustained when struck by two shells, Capercaillie immediately turned round for a second voyage to France, this time fetching home 131 soldiers, among them several wounded. Captain McKenzie himself sustained wounds from machine gun fire.

The participation of a Scottish ship in the Dunkirk evacuation was well publicized in the English press, bringing McKenzie plenty of public praise – and outright condemnation from the NPS-Labour Government in Edinburgh.

According to Scotland's (mis-)rulers, by flagrant disregard of Scotland's neutrality McKenzie had exposed all Scotland's merchant ships to possible retaliation by the Germans. Nicholas MacKerrel, our head of government, actually called in Germany's Ambassador and apologized to him for McKenzie's actions. All owners of Scotland's seagoing vessels were forthwith ordered to do nothing that could be construed as either active or passive assistance to England in the war that was 'her responsibility but not ours'.

Withdrawal of licences and the confiscation of any ship breaching this instruction were threatened as penalties.

Alongside this news, not just the English but many American papers too carried Captain McKenzie's words: 'Whit kin' o' a man wad that be, who wad staun' by and watch when his neighbour needed a haun'? Ah'll tell ye: no kin' o' a man at all'.

More than a week later, Capercaillie put into Leith with the cargo she had since loaded at Tilbury. She was greeted by a throng estimated at three thousand-plus, noisy as a football crowd, all anxious to cheer McKenzie and his crew.

A public that had once believed separation from England a good idea was beginning to see the light.

With France occupied and England left to face Germany on her own, many public voices were raised demanding that Scotland end her neutrality and give England what support she could with those meagre forces at her disposal.

Some called for the immediate introduction of conscription. Letters to newspapers showed the depth of such feelings.

Nicholas MacKerrel's response consisted of an assurance in the Edinburgh Parliament that Scotland's neutrality was inviolable. For the NPS, pacifism was an article of faith, almost a mind-deadening ideology in itself.

In any case, Hitler was now Josef Stalin's ally, and what the venerated Comrade Stalin deemed correct had the authority of infallible canon.

At Fort George, we discussed England's situation long and hard. The first instinct of most of us was to resign our commissions and offer our services to the English.

Older officers warned against this. We might yet, they counselled, be needed where we were.

Having no faith at all either in the despised MacKerrel or in Herr Hitler's inclination towards restraint, we younger ones soon saw the sense of this. We were sure that, despite the examples before their eyes of Denmark, Norway, Belgium, Luxembourg and the Netherlands, MacKerrel and his starry-eyed cohorts had failed to learn that remaining neutral is not a matter that a country may choose for itself.

Neutrality is like the tango. It doesn't work without the willing and active commitment of both parties.

6

THE sound of air-cooled radial motors jolted us into reality. A half dozen three-engined, black-crossed and swastika-ed transport aircraft appeared from the east and began disgorging paratroops.

Since first light, I had been leading my platoon on an extended route march through the countryside east of Fort George. When the paratroops appeared, we were on our way back, and no more than two miles from battalion headquarters.

We stopped almost in mid-stride, watched the dark figures tumble from the machines, saw the parachutes bloom above them, and knew that our lives were on the point of attaining their purpose.

There was no need for me to shout any order. Without exception, my men flew back in spontaneous stampede towards our quarters. On our route march we carried no weapons. Some of these were in our barracks, the remainder and the ammunition for them in stores a couple of hundred yards beyond regimental HQ.

Up and down hillocks we flew, smashed through heather, leaped over ditches and burns. I had done a fair bit of cross-country running and had always fancied myself as a middle-distance competitor. Two of my men were just as fast. On the difficult terrain, the three of us were pulling away from the rest, but still far from our quarters, when already the first of the paratroops were on the ground. The Junkers transports had turned southwards and all but vanished. Were they planning to land at Montrose, where there was an old Great War aerodrome, or would they carry on to Edinburgh?

The precision of the Germans' landing was remarkable. Their drop had been centred on our HQ buildings. As far as we could judge, the complements of all six machines touched down within an area no more than two hundred yards or so wide.

If this was the standard of German operations, no wonder France had fallen so rapidly. We were fascinated, but not mesmerized.

It was the first time, outside Warner Bros gangster pictures, that we had heard submachine guns. We knew that Germany's paratroop forces carried these most modern weapons, and had received illustrated lectures on them.

Now we knew the sound of them as well, and they were being fired at our regimental comrades.

The awareness put an extra spurt into every man's legs.

Rifle fire came from HQ in response, and for the next several minutes there was a steady concerto of individual .303 shots backed by bursts of German automatic fire.

While the lethal music cracked and rolled across the broad terrain of Fort George, we ran and ran, with only the tops of twelve-foot grassy banks in our sights. These were the embankments that stood like walls around our weapons and ammunition stores. They had been thrown up as shields against accidents. Fuming and helpless without weapons, we raced in frenzy while the numbers of our comrades' rifle reports, like the autumn days in a popular romantic song, dwindled down to a precious few. A final flurry of submachine gun fire, and we heard the rifles no more.

I and my men were hurling ourselves forward in a fury now. The three of us leading the dash had neared to around fifty yards from our weapons stores when bursts of automatic fire there brought us to an immediate halt. We all dropped to the ground, seeking what cover there was behind hillocks and bushes. The Germans knew their business. Practically the first thing they had done must have been to surround our stores. I picked myself up, zigzagged on for another twenty yards or so and peered through some dense whins.

Five of our regimental comrades lay dead outside the earth banks that surrounded the stores. Their blood was still soaking into the ground. No weapons lay near them or in their hands. They had evidently been cut down as they tried to collect arms. A German, head down so that his face was hidden under his paratrooper's helmet, was changing the magazine on his submachine gun. Two others, standing tall and vigilant, were sweeping the landscape in all directions, both with their eyes and with their weapons.

After the din of firing from both sides, the silence now held a suggestion of horror. Surely our CO had not surrendered the garrison?

The alternative picture that rose in my consciousness was scarcely less appalling. I imagined our comrades in and around regimental HQ, dead to a man, lying in their blood like the five here at the stores.

Either way, there was nothing that I and my platoon could accomplish without weapons. If we could join another garrison...

Scotland's forces were so small that the nearest regiment we could reach was stationed at Stirling Castle, a matter of 140 miles away. To Maryhill Barracks in Glasgow, home of the Highland Light Infantry, the distance was 170 miles.

The Germans must have landed at both of these locations. If they had not, it would be one of the craziest omissions in the history of warfare.

There was only one thing I could tell my platoon. 'Make your way home as best you can, and await orders. Any chance you have of acquiring a shotgun or any other weapon, take it'.

We crawled, we flew, we vaulted, we did whatever was necessary to leave the terrain of Fort George without being detected. Once on the high road, I called the platoon together. 'Try as far as possible to go by different routes. Do not go together in groups. If you do have to follow the same path as someone else, try to leave about ten minutes interval between the two of you. Make your way as far as possible singly and at intervals'.

I myself should not set off until all were on their way.

Before we parted, I shook the hand of every man. We wished each other luck, and left for our different destinations no doubt with our own differing thoughts. Mine revolved round the fate of our regimental comrades. What had happened to them? Surrender or slaughter?

The possibility at which I grasped was that our comrades, unable to reach their ammunition stores, had fought with what little stock of ammunition they had available to them. Only when that ran out were they compelled to cease fire and submit to the invaders. Submit? There might be a local victory here and there for Hitler's forces, but submit was not what Scotland was going to do.

No one was going to come in from outside and succeed in foisting his rule upon us. We were used to choosing our own rulers, and from our own people. Even Robert the Bruce was expressly warned in writing, in the Declaration of Arbroath, that he would remain King of Scots only as long as he defended his country and people. Should he fail to do so, we should 'exert ourselves at once to drive him out as our enemy and a subverter of his own rights and ours, and make our King some other man who was well able to defend us'.

The Germans might have taken Fort George, but what was happening elsewhere in Scotland? Had Hitler's Navy occupied Scapa Flow? Sailed up the Firth of Clyde into the dockyards of Glasgow?

Where else would his forces have landed? Edinburgh, to drive out the government, no doubt. Not a loss to mourn, we might have thought only yesterday. Yet whatever its manifold shortcomings, the administration in Edinburgh was *our* government. We did not want a régime imposed by Hitler.

Clearly, occupation of Scotland had one simple and direct purpose. Hitler's armies were to invade England from the north. A cross-channel invasion was likely to founder on the superiority of the Royal Navy, not to mention the destructive air attacks that would be mounted on invasion vessels by the RAF.

Paratroops? It seemed probable that Germany had not enough of these to invade England by air. An airborne invasion of Scotland, presumably from Norway, had been a much easier proposition, and a fine example of the strategy of indirect approach.

German forces now had a good springboard for penetration into the north of England – a move that would divide English forces into northern and southern elements, weakening the defences that could be mounted on any particular front.

7

I KNEW at once the route that I should take. There was no knowing which towns were already in German hands, and I was determined to bypass Inverness.

My first goal would be Fort William and the West coast, but I should not do the obvious thing and follow the Great Glen along the shore of Loch Ness. There was a quieter route to the east of the loch that led directly to its southern tip. From there a further day's march would bring me to Fort William.

Never mind the name. Fort William was no military stronghold any more, but nonetheless an important centre that the Germans were sure to occupy sooner or later. I had to pass the town and carry on southwards along the west coast without running into any Nazi patrols.

I struck out across country, stepped over the Inverness to Nairn railway line and skirted the edge of Drumossie Muir, site of the 1746 Battle of Culloden. To date, this had been the last battle fought on British soil.

If there were to be more real battles to come, I should be surprised. Our starry-eyed politicians had not maintained sufficient forces for Scotland to put an army into the field. It was to be guerrilla warfare for us, a lonely, protracted struggle pitting farmers' shotguns against the most modern weaponry on the planet. Heaven alone knew what the human cost and the outcome might be.

As was usual on route marches, the men of my platoon had been trousered. I alone wore a kilt. This was not a matter dictated by regulations, but merely my own preference.

Now the circumstance gave me two fortunate advantages. First, I was better equipped for wading through water and drying off afterwards. Second, I had a sgian dubh in my sock.

How dearly I should have loved to spring with my sgian dubh at one of the Germans now guarding our weapons stores!

Of course I should have been cut down before I had covered a tenth of the distance to the nearest man.

When I did spring into action, I should make sure that the invaders paid for my life before they took it.

By mid-afternoon I had put several miles of Highland scenery behind me. Somewhere near Strathnairn Forest I asked at a small farmhouse whether I could buy the ingredients of a meal.

Then and there I was placed at a table and fed.

I was anxious to learn any news of the German invasion, but the farmer had no wireless set.

'Ah'm told we wouldna hear onything here, onyway, because o' the hills', he explained.

He and his wife took my report of the German landing with equanimity.

'Weel, whit d'ye expect', the man wanted to know, 'when the gov'ment runs the country doon like this? We should hae stayed wi' England'.

I was interested in the man's view that the country had been run down since becoming independent, and asked him what he meant by this.

'Hae ye no noticed how a'thing's dearer since we broke awa'?' he responded.

Dearer or not, the couple refused any payment for the meal, even sending me on my way with a ham and a home-made loaf.

I spent that night on a hillside under the cover of trees. Before I slept, I thought about the farmer and his wife. The man had a shotgun, but I should not have taken it from him for the world. He might well need it yet, to defend that wife of his. For me, there would be other chances to pick up a firearm.

When I woke just before dawn next morning, I was restored and wonderfully awake but at the same time, as is usual after an al fresco Highland night, cold in body and limb.

The simplest of remedies was readily available.

I buckled on my kilt and set off at an allegro tempo towards the far end of Loch Ness. Bodily, I was very soon warmed up to normal working temperature. In mind I was already overheated. Less than twenty-four hours had passed since the German landing. What damage might the invaders already have done, what casualties might they by now have inflicted on our poor misled people?

That simple farmer whose wife had fed me yesterday had hit the nail squarely on the head. 'We should hae stayed wi' England'. Here was an unpretentious soul, unmistakably hard working, whose life was filled with little beyond facing up to realities squarely. It was evident that he asked for nothing beyond what he earned by his own exertion, and he certainly would have no time for fancy theories or dogma. Self-delusion would be the very last sin to which such a man would fall prey.

'We should hae stayed wi' England'. Ceart gu leòr, as they say in the Gaelic. Right enough.

The tragedy now unfolding in these islands had been made possible by wishful thinking, short-sightedness, self-obsession and failure both to think the matter through and to appreciate the lessons of history.

Well, we were being given a lesson now that it would be difficult to ignore. How many Scots men and women would have to die and suffer before it finally sank in that the peoples of these islands could defend themselves better when united and – most importantly – could plan and prepare for any necessary defence far better through a single central government with combined resources? The added strength of unity would mean that they could deter, and deterrence is always the better and cheaper option than war, both in material terms and in its human cost. Separated, each country would always be weaker, would fail to deter and become easier prey.

Oh, no doubt there are many internal matters that might be administered better for the Scottish people by a government in Edinburgh. What should be the extent of these powers, which areas of government they should cover, I am unqualified to say. One thing I do know: Foreign affairs and defence should not be among them.

Reflecting on these matters occupied me until the day's first sunlight showed the southern end of Loch Ness to be within an hour's march. It was time to concentrate on looking out for Germans.

As the hill dropped down towards the loch, I studied the ground until locating suitable cover from which I could observe, without being seen, all movement on the shores and in the village of Fort Augustus. Yes, another fort, this one dating from the first Jacobite rising but now in the hands of the Benedictine order and converted, so I had heard, into an abbey. Ten minutes later I crossed to the whins I had selected as cover and settled down for a lengthy watch. Higher up on the hillside I had picked out two possible lines of retreat.

A mast was moving above the rooftops of the village. A yacht was travelling the Caledonian Canal, which ran from Inverness to Fort William via Loch Ness, Loch Oich and Loch Lochy. The vessel stopped for several minutes before moving onwards. She had been put through the canal locks.

That settled it. There were no Germans here yet. If there had been, they would have taken charge of the locks and have stopped the yacht.

I rose from my hiding place and started down the hillside at an angle, so as to reach canal level comfortably past Fort Augustus.

So far the land appeared clear, but I was taking no chances and should certainly have to move away from the canal well before arriving at Fort William. I pressed on away from the road, parallel to Loch Oich, all the while looking far ahead along the water and the road to see what might be moving inland.

The sun was more or less at its highest by the time I reached Laggan Locks. Here a stretch of canal connects Loch Oich to Loch Lochy.

Before nearing Spean Bridge I took to the hillside and bedded down on the comfort of heather and in the shelter of ferns. I had marched through much of the preceding night, as well as having been on the move all day. Sleep came almost on the instant.

As soon as sun woke me, I started moving along close enough to Fort William to be able to keep the town in view. It was not long before I became aware that the ground I was covering was becoming the lower slopes of Ben Nevis. I had no wish to go too high, yet was determined to keep Fort William under observation before moving down into the town. If I ventured into the town.

I stayed well up from the road and passed behind every bush or object that would shield me from eyes down below. Keeping up higher than the road and the water was a two-edged sword. I avoided running into all whom I might not wish to meet, and would be able to identify these from a distance. At the same time, a single figure like myself moving across a hillside would be easily detected from below.

The smooth outlines of Fort William's aluminium smelter, opened only some ten years earlier, caught my attention before any features of the town became apparent. This was my signal to ca' canny, as the Highlander says.

For that last mile I moved from wall to hedge, from trees to hillock.

There might so far be no enemy at all in this part of the country, but the exercise of proper caution would at the very least be invaluable practice for the difficult times that I knew were to come.

If I could avoid the eyes of my fellow countrymen who, being familiar with the terrain, did not miss anything unusual, I ought to be able to evade the sight of an invader.

Passing below the smelter, I was able to distinguish above the roofs of the town the masts of fishing boats and yachts in the Caledonian Canal basin.

Above these masts rose another, much taller and with a high crossbeam. A navy ship! Not ours, surely. Scotland's navy, almost non-existent, was risible. And if this were a visitor, then only English or German.

A pennant hung from the topmost point of the mast, but without wind to display it I could distinguish none of its colours.

An open truck bearing the name of a local contractor came towards me along the road leading to the smelter. I ducked behind a dry stone dyke. Seated in the open back of the truck were perhaps a dozen soldiers whose coal scuttle style helmets told me everything. The truck stopped at the gatehouse of the smelter. A man – an ordinary, glorious man – stepped out of the gatehouse with a shotgun, and fired both barrels through the windscreen at the helmeted driver. A soldier in the back of the truck stood up and shot the man immediately.

The German driver was dead. Soldiers jumped down from the vehicle, tugging at the bolts of the weapons in their hands. An officer who had been sitting next to the driver leaped out of the cab and ordered men into the smelter. They reappeared pushing or dragging workers with them. The officer counted the captives and sent two soldiers back into the works. These returned with two more employees. There were now nine Scots in the soldiers' hands. One, clearly an apprentice, looked no older than a schoolboy. Two, completely grey haired, must have been nearing retirement.

The officer ordered all nine placed against the factory wall. The same number of soldiers lined up at once, no more than five yards from the men. They took immediate aim. The officer raised and lowered his arm.

Hillside echoes reinforced the volley. The whiteness of the wall made the bullet chips blacker, the smears and spurts of blood more crimson.

The German officer stepped from body to body to fire a single pistol shot into each head. His pistol held only eight shots, and to finish the job he had to change the magazine. The ninth man was clearly dead, but received his coup de grâce just the same. Including the man with the shotgun, ten Scotsmen had been killed, the number of hostages allowed under the Hague Convention for the life of every enemy serviceman killed by a civilian.

Leaving two soldiers outside to deal with the body of his driver, the German officer led the rest of his men into the smelter. I watched the two Germans lay their dead driver on the floor of the open truck, then clear the shattered windscreen.

Under guard, a group of workers emerged from the works carrying shovels. More by gesticulation than language, their German escorts ordered them to remove their dead workmates a little way down the hillside and to bury them.

It was time for me to move on.

These Germans were no paratroopers, but commonplace infantry. They did not wear the abbreviated paratroop helmet but the familiar coal scuttle. Nor were they equipped with those deadly submachine guns, carrying instead the bolt action rifle that had seen them through the Great War. It was apparent that they had landed from the ship whose mast top I could see.

Had she sailed in alone? If not, how many other vessels might there be in the invasion party?

Fort William was barred to me. And how far into the surrounding Lochaber countryside might the invaders already have penetrated? There was nothing for it. I should just have to skirt round the foothills of Ben Nevis some way higher up than I had intended. My plan from the beginning had been to make for Fort William and head down the West coast from there. Down the coast I should still have to go, but now the various narrow passages, the ferry at Ballachulish, the crossing or skirting of Loch Creran, the railway bridge at Connel, would all presumably be in German hands.

To reach Fort William, the German troop carrier would have had to sail the entire length of Loch Linnhe from the open sea. Surely she would have put ashore detachments of soldiers at various locations where she had to pass through narrows. Nowhere along my proposed coastal route would be safe. It took me three hours to work my way from the aluminium smelter, past the town, until I found myself part way up Glen Nevis. Where I should go from the head of the glen, I had no idea, but it struck me that here, after all, was the way to go. Inland, over the mountains, rather than parallel to a coastline that was sure to be kept under German eyes.

There were plenty of people, I knew, who enjoyed climbing mountains. I was not one of them. All the same, I was young and fit. All I had to do was make the effort. I plodded a couple of miles up the glen and collapsed, exhausted, in the shelter of a tiny copse.

The rain woke me a little after 3am. It was heavy and soaked my kilt pretty thoroughly before I had chance to react. Apart from this, the first effect it had on me was to make me realize how fortunate I had been in having had dry weather for my first three days of travel.

Had it been only three days? Three days of hiking for me, and three days of German occupation for my country. This, I knew, was only the beginning. How many people were there in thinly populated areas who, like the farmer and his wife at Strathnairn Forest, had no wireless set and no idea of what was happening?

With the downpour showing no sign of slackening, there seemed no sense in continuing to lie down under it on ground that was becoming more waterlogged by the minute. Saturated as it was, I pulled my kilt round me and set off along the road leading up the glen. Water was running down the road in a shallow but fast torrent stretching from one side to the other.

Some forty minutes or so of trudging head down through what seemed like a solid wall of water, and there it was. A wooden log store, not far off the road. Behind it a cottage, in total darkness. If I had only kept going last night, I should have come across the log store and enjoyed a dry, full night's sleep. I let myself in to the wooden construction, stripped off and stretched out. Expectations of more sleep proved illusory. There were sacks in the store, and I placed a couple of them on the floor to provide a smooth surface. Even with these, and another two covering myself, I was simply too far chilled through to be able to drift away into unconsciousness. Apart from this, rain hammering on the roof of my refuge was an incessant bar to oblivion.

I was lost and stumbling through that no man's land between the front lines of sleep and wakefulness when one of my more alert brain sentinels became part aware of movement and sound outside. The door of the store opened, and a fine Highland tongue uttered a single imprecation. In the next instant, a short, strongly built man whose clothes glistened from head to foot with water took one rapid step inside and seized a pitchfork from its place in a corner.

'A' richt, ye scunner, let's hae ye, an' nane o' your Nazi tricks, mind'.

8

ON the instant I was fully awake. In other circumstances I might have laughed at being taken for a German, but was still too exhausted and cold to do more than protest my Scottishness and indicate the kilt, tunic, socks and other appurtenances which I had spread out in the faint hope of their drying.

'Weel' - the man was far from convinced – 'ye may be, or ye may no' be whit ye say. Ye'll come intae the hoose, an' we'll tak' a look at ye'.

At least this man had heard of the invasion and was on his toes. Good.

Under the man's mistrustful scrutiny, I slipped my bare feet into my still soaking brogues, scooped up everything else and preceded the man with the pitchfork from wood store to cottage. I was thankful to see not only that lights were burning inside, but that a 'healthy ribbon of smoke was pushing upwards from chimney into rain.

'Jenny!' called the man, reaching past me to open the cottage door. 'Hae ye same dry claes for this visitor o' oors?'

Within three minutes I was seated by the most wonderful log fire that I had ever seen, wearing a shirt and dungarees that were much too small for me but that had the exquisite merit of being both dry and warm.

Despite his initial and understandable mistrust, it was obvious that the man, whose name was Ferguson, now accepted me as genuine. This became apparent when he left me alone with his wife while he went out to fetch in the logs that had been the original reason for his going out to the store.

Before Ferguson returned, I was sitting before a mug of steaming tea and a bowl of porage that would have done credit to the breakfast table of a titan.

While I ate, Mrs Ferguson, a motherly, jolly soul, busied herself with my clothing. Clouds of steam were soon rising from my kilt, shirt, tunic and socks, arrayed round the fire. Pages from newspapers, screwed up and forced tightly into my brogues, completed the efforts at drying out my kit.

The Fergusons had learned of the invasion from their wireless set, and I was anxious to hear the latest news. Scottish broadcasting stations were no use. Without exception, these had been taken over by the Germans, who were using them to spread misleading propaganda and issue orders. It was forbidden on pain of death to keep firearms or ammunition. All shotguns and other weapons were to be handed in to the local Kommandantur or to the nearest German Army unit. A strict curfew was to be enforced. After one hour before sunset no one was to be outside his home without the express permission of the local commander. All public meetings were henceforth forbidden. No groups of more than three persons were to meet in any public place. Travel was restricted. No private cars were to be allowed on the roads. And so on and so on.

All of this was reinforced by talks from Lord Haw-Haw, congratulating the Scottish people on the glorious part they had already played and were yet further to play in overthrowing the 'hypocritical and self-seeking rule' of the English over their nearest neighbours.

Only from the BBC, down in England, were trustworthy news reports to be heard. Parliament in Edinburgh and Maryhill Barracks in Glasgow had both been taken through paratroop actions followed by seaborne landings. The Scottish

Government had been arrested. Stranraer, Fort William, Inverness, Stirling, the Orkneys and the Shetlands had all fallen into German hands.

I had heard enough. No point trying to locate an intact Scots garrison.

Yet no mention so far of the Western Isles. This must surely follow.

So far the Germans had done an amazing amount in a very short time. If we had not learned it before, through those newsreels from the Continent, we knew now what Blitzkrieg meant.

That day's rain was of the sort, well known throughout the Highlands, that seems to have a mandate to go on and on and never to stop.

Of course it always does stop some time. That day's slowed down in the early afternoon, then faded over the next hour into nothing.

My clothes were dry enough to wear. My brogues, though, remained decidedly damp on the inside. All the same, I was desperate to press on.

Many times since, I have had occasion to think back to the Fergusons, as also to the couple at Strathnairn, whose name I never learned. What might have happened to them, isolated in an otherwise empty landscape, totally vulnerable whenever the Germans should arrive at their doors?

Like that other couple, the Fergusons too saw me off with food – enough for two days. I doubted that they could spare so much, and also felt some guilt at leaving them to the mercies of whatever troops might soon come up the glen.

Even so, there were still some hours of daylight to go, and I knew that I should waste none of them.

Water was still running down the road as I set off. Not a torrent now, nonetheless sufficient testimony to the volume yet to leave the slopes of rock above. To my left as I mounted the glen, the mass of Ben Nevis seemed to overpower the whole landscape. I had set myself the objective of going as high as possible before stopping for the night. I had instructions from Ferguson, and knew that a mile or so ahead, where the glen took a sharp turn to the left, I should leave the road to follow upwards the course of a burn that ran down the shoulder of one of the higher mountains in the region. Once I had crossed that shoulder, I should be able to come down the other side directly to Kinlochleven. That would cut out the need for the risky Ballachulish ferry.

I did not deceive myself about the demands that this climb would make on my stamina, and planned to bed down in good time so as to conserve strength for the morning.

In the event, I made better progress than I had anticipated. I found a hollow below the summit of my climb, where I slept well out of the winds that would have assailed me had I gone higher.

As so often after a rain-filled day, the following morning was one of glorious blue and dazzling sun. I was at the peak of my climb in very few minutes, and paused for a moment to enjoy the panorama below. Loch Leven with its pattern of shadows and glitter, beyond it the hills of Glencoe and farther still the emptiness of Rannoch Moor.

As on my way up, I was able heading down the mountainside to follow the course of a burn.

I had gone perhaps half way down, when a bush not forty yards from me sprang into sudden life. From it careered a stag. The beast shot obliquely across my path and rocketed down the hillside at an angle, followed by five other deer.

To anyone looking up the hill, this would have been a certain indication of human presence. This was a severe warning, if ever there were one. I went to ground and stayed motionless for a half hour before moving on. Only now did it occur to me how easy it was to advertise my presence. Way back before reaching Fort William, I had startled a couple of grouse, and foolishly thought nothing of it. From now on I should watch out for sensitive wildlife just as sharply as for Germans.

I had not eaten before setting off. Once I was within five minutes' walk of the lochside and Kinlochleven, I settled down behind an outcrop of ferns, from where I could study the village, and set about making a late breakfast. Not a hundred yards from me, the waterfall known as the Grey Mare's Tail provided an incessant background thunder as the water leaped for fully fifty yards to the rocks below.

The roar of the cataract all but smothered the rifle crack. The shot had come from down below me.

Two German soldiers appeared from the grounds of a cottage on the lochside. Besides his rifle, each carried a shotgun. In addition, one held a bag of the sort used by gamekeepers to carry ammunition.

At Kinlochleven the Scottish (formerly British) Aluminium Company had yet another smelter. Indeed, these works had been the reason for the foundation of this village.

The soldiers marched past the spot where I was keeping watch, and disappeared towards the smelter. The works were presumably their unit's base in the village. These two had been out to collect firearms and had shot a gun owner who had resisted confiscation.

I gave it five minutes after the Germans had disappeared, before slipping down the rest of the way to the road. Sure enough, a middle-aged man in shirtsleeves lay dead on the ground outside the cottage that the soldiers had left.

I went in to the man and straightened his limbs. I left him lying decently on his back, arms folded over his chest. For the rest, I regretted that I should have to leave it to his neighbours to bury him.

One way or another, I had to reach the south bank of Loch Leven. This meant either using the ferry at Ballachulish, well down towards the sea entrance to the loch, or simply turning round the head of the water onto the south side, right here in the village. Going through the village, though, would surely mean passing within sight of the Germans at the smelter. Yet would the ferry be any safer? Just as surely as occupying the smelter, the Germans must have taken over the ferry as well, for moving their own men and vehicles.

This left me effectively stymied. Of course, there were alternatives. I could try to swim the loch, or I could steal a rowing boat. This is what the hero in a fictional story would do.

To be frank, I am no Richard Hannay. Nor am I a Bulldog Drummond. I was always one of the poorest swimmers in my regiment, and should give little for my chances against the currents that I knew were lurking beneath the surface of the water stretching away before me. Still, I am an experienced rower and could make short work of the crossing. Provided, of course, that the Germans had not commandeered every dinghy along the loch shores. It was certainly a fact that I could see no vessel of any kind anywhere along the stretch of Loch Leven that was within my view.

I sat for a half hour watching both the village and that part of the loch plied by the Ballachulish ferry. In Kinlochleven, nobody stirred. Not a figure showed itself in the street or in a garden. No vehicle, not even a bicycle, appeared on the lochside road.

I began to study the terrain behind and above the houses and the smelter. No route that I could take to circumvent the village would be entirely without risk, but this was of course no more than to be expected. I narrowed my choice of paths down to two, deciding to make a final choice according to what I might encounter once I was on my way.

The explosion put a momentary end to my thinking. It shut out the roar of the Grey Mare's Tail. It covered much of Kinlochleven with black cloud. It set off a wave of echoes rolling back and forth from mountainside to mountainside.

The aluminium smelter had gone up in an instant ballooning of orange and red fire.

9

HAD the Germans decided to destroy the smelter? No, surely not. Our own people must have sabotaged the works in order to deny it to the Germans. An act of defiance.

How many more such acts might there have been already during the few days that the Germans had been here? How many more might there not be to come?

Well done, those smelter workers who had done this thing! Well done, even though it was certain to bring down retribution on the people of the village.

Sabotage of this kind had been easy enough for anyone from Kinlochleven. Just down the road at Ballachulish was a quarry. And a quarry offers the most easily accessible source of dynamite.

Once the black clouds had dissipated, it was clear that the smelter had been wrecked from one end to the other. This ruled out a single explosion. Dynamite had clearly been deployed at several places. Whoever had wrecked the smelter had not stinted on his materials. Altogether, there must have been a massive amount of explosive brought to detonation.

This was no occasion to waste time. The Germans would be here very soon. All the soldiers who had been in the smelter were, one hoped, dead. It would not take others long to arrive from Fort William – or from Ballachulish ferry, if there were indeed troops there.

I pushed myself to my feet and strode off towards the village. Fragments of metal walls and roof from the smelter lay on the road and in gardens. Villagers were not to be seen.

Along the north shore of the loch, a car was racing towards the village. The Ballachulish ferry was moored at its landing stage on the north shore, which told me what I needed to know. Germans from the ferry were on their way to investigate the explosion.

I dived behind the garden wall of the last house until the car had disappeared towards the smoking factory.

The important thing was to keep out of sight of whoever was left at the ferry. Moving at a good pace along the south shore of the loch, I reached the entrance to Glencoe without encountering a soul. Barely a mile farther on, and still a good two miles from the ferry, I turned away from the loch into a glen that I knew would lead me into Creran Forest. It was across country or nothing. The coast road was where any Germans would be moving, and all crossings of sea lochs – I still had Loch Creran and Loch Etive ahead of me – would be under guard.

This was an easier trek than I had made on the previous day. I should have nothing like the same height to climb before reaching the head of Loch Etive. A further spring was put into my paces by the memory of the sight and sound of the Kinlochleven sabotage. My countrymen were going to take nothing lying down!

Not that I had ever thought for a moment that they would, but this almost immediate act, coming on only the fifth day of occupation, was triumphant proof of their unconquerable spirit and resolution.

Loch Creran I was able to bypass on the landward side. Before reaching the head of the loch I arrived at Glen Ure, very flat to begin with, but then climbing sharply. Cutting across to my right when past the head of the glen, I found the course of the burn that would lead me down almost to the head of Loch Etive.

It was here that I bedded down on heather. Thinking over the events of that day kept me awake for an hour or more, yet sleep came in the end and I did not wake until it was again fully light.

Last lap now. Late tonight, if I really stepped out, I should be at my mother's house outside Oban.

Turning around the head of Loch Etive onto the south bank was simple enough. The ground was flat until I ran into a stretch where the hillside ran straight down into the water without any bank. This made for tricky going for a couple of miles. Then the terrain flattened out again, and I was able to speed up. There was even a track of sorts as I came nearer to Ben Cruachan.

Ahead were the Glasgow to Oban railway line, the village of Taynuilt and the Bonawe Iron Works. Beyond the foundry, the Bonawe ferry ran a very short distance across the loch to its northern shore. I was relieved to note that the ferry boat, as at Ballachulish, was currently at the northern bank. Were the Germans over there? Surely not. They must be here, occupying the iron works, which they would expect to press into service for themselves.

I knew this area fairly well, and so had a clear idea of how I should approach my mother's home. To pass well behind the iron works and also to skirt Taynuilt, I took to the trees that fringed the lower slopes of Ben Cruachan. The wood covered me right up to the railway line.

Just beyond the line, running parallel to the rails, was the main road to Oban. This would take me home, but naturally I intended to travel across country instead.

I peeped out from between the trees, and looked both ways along the railway line. Nothing. No train, no human being in sight.

I wasted no time in leaping the tracks and going to ground alongside the road. A cautious survey. No one in sight here, either.

Crouching, I moved alongside the road until I was opposite a wood. I should disappear into this, make my way westwards well away from the Oban road and vanish farther on into Fearnoch Forest. Once I emerged from the trees onto clear ground south of the Black Lochs, I should then have only a mile or so more to reach my mother's home.

I rose and stepped onto the road. So, from the other side, did a German paratrooper, SMG pointing at my head.

The German sauntered towards me, taking in my now dishevelled uniform with its lieutenant's shoulder pips.

'So', he sneered, 'a Scottish officer. And running away. This is not what the Führer told us about Scotsmen in his book'.

The man was paying more attention to his own amusement than to keeping his eye on me and his hands firmly on the weapon he was holding. He had been careless, too, in approaching to within five feet of his prisoner. I swooped down for the sgian dubh in my right sock.

Of course I did not deserve to survive that movement, and it was only the million to one freak of a dud round that saved me in defiance of my deserts.

Even through my tunic sleeve I could feel the warmth of the German's blood that spurted onto my arm from the sgian dubh in his throat. The paratrooper's eyes rolled upwards and he was dead soon after hitting the ground.

I had his submachine gun, and it had no defects. That was all that mattered. I dragged the German's body off the road and rolled it into the trees where he had been hiding. I suppose he must have seen me before I entered the cover of the wood alongside Ben Cruachan, and simply been watching and waiting for me ever since. On his belt, the man had another, full magazine of thirty two nine-millimetre rounds. I tucked this away.

The dead paratrooper had not arrived here alone. Very probably his unit had commandeered the ancient Taynuilt Hotel, which has sheltered travellers for several centuries. Doubtless these Germans will have been the first not to have been accorded the usual Highland welcome. Taynuilt was an obvious target for early capture by paratroops because it offered control of the Pass of Brander, a main east-west link. In all probability it would not be long before his comrades discovered the paratrooper's body, which was uncovered and lay barely six feet from the road.

Villagers from Taynuilt would then be rounded up and shot in retaliation.

Along with everything else in my possession, the notebook in my tunic pocket had suffered badly from the hours of rain. Its pages, mostly stuck together, had since dried after a fashion. I found a page that was usable, and took out my fountain pen.

'To the Commander of the German Paratroopers at Taynuilt', I wrote. 'This afternoon I killed one of your men in combat. You will find his body about a mile outside the village alongside the main Glasgow to Oban road (on the south side). I must emphasize that your comrade's death was due to my own actions alone. NO civilian whatsoever was involved. This was a confrontation between two uniformed soldiers, and no one else was present. When your comrade attempted to fire on me, his weapon jammed due to a dud round. I enclose this round as evidence. I had no firearm, and killed your comrade with my sgian dubh, or black knife, which is a normal part of a Highland regiment's uniform'.

I signed this with my full name, rank and number, specifying my regiment and adding that I had escaped from Fort George when paratroops had captured the garrison. If the Germans would take the trouble to check with Fort George, they would be satisfied as to my identity. Whether they would take this trouble, and whether even if they did they would spare the villagers, there was of course no means of knowing. I could only pray that their commander was a civilized man who recognized and abided by the acknowledged rules of war.

I folded the notebook page as neatly as I could around the dud nine-millimetre cartridge. The result was something of the size and shape of a small cigar. For a soldier, the indentation on the percussion cap was unmistakable. This was clearly a dud round, and equally obviously one of the same manufacture as those carried by German paratroopers. They could not doubt my story.

What faced me now was the problem of delivering my message. I spent something approaching half an hour working my way round the back of Taynuilt village and through to the side of the hotel. Halfway along the frontage of the building, the entrance porch was guarded by a single paratrooper, his SMG slung on its leather strap over a shoulder. This confirmed to me that the hotel was indeed the seat of the local Kommandantur.

I stepped round the corner of the building and began to walk towards the sentry, holding the SMG that I had taken from the dead paratrooper. I was about to call a challenge when the German, hearing my footsteps, swivelled on his feet to face me. His SMG swung into the firing position faster than I should have thought possible.

I had no choice. A brief compression of the trigger, and a short burst of fire sent the German whirling backwards to the ground. I ran the last few yards, placed my 'letter' on the dead man's chest, tugged the SMG from his hands and flew from the scene back into the woods.

10

AT every stride I expected to be struck in the back by a burst of fire, but of course I was soon among the houses of the village and the Germans would have no sight of me. Yet with the advantage of numbers, the Germans would quickly be able to surround the woods and cover every exit. They could beat their way through the trees at will. There was nowhere for me to go.

Well, I had at least reduced the number of the occupying forces by two, and should eliminate a few more of them before they finally downed me.

Through the trees I stumbled on and on, well conscious that I was leaving my pursuers the easiest of trails to follow. Finally I stopped and looked back along the way that I had come.

My trail was not all that obvious. To a Red Indian, yes, but not to common or garden European soldiery, surely. And I had been running for how long? These woods must be far bigger than I had anticipated. The odds were not all on the German side, after all.

It struck me with a rush that I had a tremendous thirst. My mouth was so dry that my tongue was cleaving to the roof. What was left of the food given me by the Fergusons was in my tunic pockets. I should not go hungry, but thirst was a different and a desperate matter, particularly after great exertion. I had spent perhaps an hour running at top speed. Now I must find a way out of these woods and go in search of water.

Leaving the woods was unnecessary. Within a few hundred yards I stumbled on a burn running between the trees. The water was clear, and deep enough for me to scoop adequate handfuls. I had no water bottle, which was something that I should have to rectify. I could eat, though, at least for today.

As abruptly as I had been assailed by thirst, it came to me that I was tired. Very tired. It had after all been quite a day. I had encountered my first two Germans face to face, and killed them both.

It had also not occurred to me what a distance I had covered since waking. I did not feel that I could go another step. I unfastened my kilt and wrapped myself in it. I did not bother about covering myself with leaves, or attempting any other sort of camouflage. I did, though, lay each of my two SMGs within close reach of my hands, facing in opposite directions.

For the first night since the invasion, I failed to have a full and proper sleep. I would doze for anything between forty and sixty minutes at a time and then wake up. Being thoroughly tired, I had no difficulty in going off again, but the repeated interruptions deprived me of the full benefit of what sleep I did have. Some time before four and five o'clock I decided that it was pointless trying to drift off again. Who knew whether German troops might not be combing through the trees towards me? I rose, washed in the burn and drank my fill of the cold, revitalizing water.

I had expected to spend that night at my mother's house, or, if not that, at least to have seen my mother before moving on. Depending on who might be blocking my path, I might still be able to call on her by tonight – only one day later than I had hoped. After that – well, there was just one decent thing to do. If there were no Scottish regiments able to carry on the fight to throw out the invader, I should try to reach the English forces and join them.

To land up at my mother's, there was no escaping the fact that ultimately I should have to relinquish the shelter of the woods and travel across open country. The sooner I started, the better.

I slung an SMG over each shoulder, and made my way out of the woods. I headed southwards, directly away from Taynuilt. Two miles brought me to a small freshwater loch. I turned westwards here, climbing the shoulder between two moderately high bens before dropping into Glen Feochain. The going here was easy, and this was a glen leading to the main road south out of Oban.

My mother's house was north of the town, and very quickly reached by an overland route, provided that no German blocked my way. There was no question of my trying to cover the distance quickly. I passed well to the landward side of the town, moving from one bit of cover to another only after exhaustive study of my surroundings.

It was late afternoon before I arrived at a point opposite my mother's home. Between me and the house ran a road, normally well used, now empty of traffic. Easy enough for the Germans to have a concealed sniper covering the spot. But why would they? Unless they had checked with their comrades at Fort George and knew my home address. And if they did, they could just as easily have a man inside the house itself.

What would be the point of my waiting? I should have to cross the road some time.

A patch of white caught my eye on a telegraph pole. It took perhaps a minute before it occurred to me that a telegraph pole was just the sort of place where the invader would place his notices, the Kommandant's orders to the occupied population.

I crept along parallel to the road until I was opposite the pole in question. Dare I spend a half minute standing still, exposed on the edge of the road, while I read the notice? Did I need to read it? Odd that it was on the pole nearest my family home. Could it be a wanted notice? Had the Germans put a price on my head after my two killings?

Curiosity won. I rose and stepped up smartly to the pole. It was not a wanted notice. It had nothing to do with my activities. Headed 'District Kommandantur' and signed 'Gehring, Major, Kommandant', it read in faultless English – and in words that I shall never forget – 'In flagrant violation of the Treaty of Neutrality concluded between the Greater German Reich and the Government of Scotland, on 12. October 1940 two German soldiers were killed by gunshot approximately two kilometres south of Dunbeg. In accordance with the terms of the Regulations Respecting the Laws and Customs of War on Land contained in the Hague Convention IV of 1907, the following persons have been executed by order of the German District Command'.

There followed a list of twenty names. One of them leaped out at me. It was the name of my mother.

11

I SWAYED, rocked on my feet. Then pulled myself together and walked straight to my mother's door. I could let myself in only by opening a kitchen window round at the back.

Let the Germans come. I was ready for them. Not only with my SMGs, but with my rage.

I had now lost both my parents to the Germans.

I pulled back the bolt of an SMG and sprang from room to room, thrusting open doors and leaping inside with my finger on the trigger.

Any German I encountered would have less than a second to live. All right, so he would be waiting for me inside, with his finger similarly on a trigger. I too would have less than a second to live. But at least I should take him with me.

No German was in the house. Of course not. If there had been, the outside doors would scarcely have been locked.

Soldiers shot near Dunbeg. That was right here, just along the road. Nothing to do with my two, then.

Yet the selection of hostages was usually a random and arbitrary affair. In this case, though, had they collected my mother because she was my mother? Had I brought this on her by confessing my first Taynuilt killing? While intending to protect civilians unknown to me, had I brought an ignominious death on my own mother instead?

I sat for at least an hour in practically total numbness. The awareness of what I had perhaps done was too horrible to contemplate. I pushed it, and everything else, from my mind, escaped into mental and emotional emptiness. Only the realization that the room was almost dark woke me into activity. Night had all but set in.

I dared not use any light, but fortunately this was unnecessary. I knew my way into the last corner not only of every room, but also of every last cupboard and cabinet.

First I made a small pot of tea. Herring were there, already coated in oatmeal. The larder held an abundance of bread and butter. What I did not eat alongside the herring I should take with me as sandwiches in the morning.

One other thing I needed besides food and drink. News. I switched on the wireless, very quietly, and noted with satisfaction that my mother had left the set tuned to the BBC. The news itself caused me less gratification. German forces, pushing south from Scotland, had encircled Berwick and already penetrated Carlisle. A rapid German thrust along the East coast was nearing a point opposite Lindisfarne, or Holy Island, as it was generally known.

In the south, RAF airfields had again been under attack from Luftwaffe bombers. So too had South Coast ports. All preparations for a cross-Channel invasion.

The sooner I could join the English forces, the better. First, needing sleep, I lay down in my old bed. I was kept awake by wondering about what I had not dared to envisage during the evening: Where had my mother's body been buried?

Tipped without reverence into a pit with the other nineteen hostages, I assumed. At least my grandparents, who had died before hostilities, had been spared this horror.

Though most of what I needed was back in my room at Fort George, by good fortune I had left some new items of uniform clothing at my mother's during my last leave. After the travels of the last few days, it was a tonic to put on a new shirt and a new pair of socks.

There was some money, several pounds, where I knew that my mother had kept an emergency sum. I took this, though frankly believing that I should never dare show myself in a shop. Not wearing my Army uniform.

I left the house by the back door, an SMG over each shoulder and the haversack of provisions slung round onto my back.

A rapid look along the road in both directions, and I was across in a flash. I went at once into cover and began working my way back along the route that I had followed yesterday. I set off with the intention of heading once more along Glen Feochain. In the event, I changed my mind and went by Glen Lonan instead.

It was scarcely a rational decision, since the continuation of this glen ran directly into Taynuilt, with its detachment of troops looking out for the killer of their two comrades. All the same, if I remained on the alert and did nothing silly, there seemed no reason to overdo the avoidance of known danger spots. Many risks simply had to be faced.

One way or another, for instance, I needed to pass the twenty-odd mile stretch of Loch Awe, that fresh water obstacle that lies like a gash in the landscape right across the path of the traveller between west and east.

Leaping across the River Awe, where it flowed from a northern arm of the loch, I dropped one of my SMGs. Wound up as I was, the splash seemed to me as loud as an explosion.

Disregarding my brogues and socks, I jumped into the water and heaved the weapon out. At battle readiness now, I crawled into some ferns and lay there listening for any indication of other human presence.

My second SMG was in my hands, with the bolt drawn back.

Ten minutes elapsed, and I heard nothing beyond the usual sounds of animals, birds and wind in the trees.

I moved on.

There is no point in my retailing every detail of my journey. Fraught with tension as it was for me, to you it can only sound repetitive. Over and over, the story as before. A lengthy slog uphill, over the shoulder between two hills, then down, down, down following the path of a burn. How I surveyed each road at length before crossing it. How I crept unseen past villages, keeping behind every scrap of cover and moving little more than a yard at a time. How I passed by Loch Lomond to the north, and, still undetected, reached the Trossachs.

Confident by now that I could see anyone climbing towards me well before he would see me, I settled onto the heather and made inroads into my stock of sandwiches.

Fortified by the contents of my whisky bottle, I struck out for Loch Katrine with some vigour. At the head of the water I was faced with a direct choice: to go along the south bank, or the north. This was no quandary. The south bank was comfortably walkable, whereas that on the north ran steeply down into the water, with no safe banking at all.

Three miles along the lochside, the unmistakable sound of an aircraft engine broke into my self-satisfaction. Almost in a panic, I dived into the heather and made frantic efforts to pull clumps of the plant over me. I was aware of an aircraft arriving from the Glasgow direction.

I looked and knew it for a Fieseler Storch, a small German monoplane that had low take-off and landing speeds and could therefore operate from even a short stretch of field.

The machine passed almost directly overhead, then dipped a wing and began to turn as though to have another look.

I unslung an SMG and pulled back the bolt.

The Fieseler put down its nose and dipped unswervingly towards me. That I had been seen was unmistakable. Two faces were looking directly at me through the windscreen.

The Fieseler was not designed to carry built-in machine guns, but there was nothing to say that this one had not been specially adapted.

The machine was very low now, and very close. I could see the eyes of the faces in the cockpit.

I emptied my SMG magazine straight into the engine nacelle.

It was the magazine that had contained the dud round, and the Fieseler took all of the remaining thirty one.

The machine burst into fire, began to wobble and dived directly at the spot where I crouched.

I put every ounce of available muscle into an effort at leaping sideways, caught a foot in the sling of the SMG and fell flat onto my face.

I began to push myself up, saw the Fieseler looming closer, watched as the wobble grew greater, swerving the machine away from me and out over the loch.

The aircraft continued to lose height. A wing tip brushed the water, dug in. The Fieseler cartwheeled, struck the surface upside down. Within a minute, every part of the aircraft disappeared into the loch.

Well, that'll put out the fire, I thought, still not on my feet.

More to the point: that was a couple more that I had on my account. I was certainly thankful that on this trip the pilot had not been alone. Or could perhaps three have climbed into such a small machine? One could only hope.

12

I WATCHED for some minutes more, but saw no one bob up from the depths. If anyone had appeared, well, I had my second SMG, thoroughly dried out now, ready for him.

If no German had been around to see the crash – which is how it looked – the aircraft's disappearance would remain a mystery to them. Let them spend countless man hours searching the countryside in vain for her.

They would be unlikely to suspect that the machine had been shot out of the sky. Unless of course her pilot had put through a radio message reporting my presence at the lochside. I considered this, though, unlikely. No experienced serviceman would make a report until he had checked and confirmed the facts. That was surely what he was trying to do when he flew back towards me.

Throughout my trek so far I had seen as good as none of my fellow countrymen. Shepherds and gamekeepers were absent from the hills, on the lochs no fishermen waited and hoped. No tractors moved in the fields or on the hillsides, no farmhands tended either to soil or to crops. Gamekeepers, of course, would be absent from our countryside for as long as the occupation lasted. The Germans would still be making it their business to visit each farm and croft, terrorizing the occupants and seeking out every last hiding place of a firearm. This systematic combing of the countryside by the invader was one of the hazards for which I was principally on my guard. No matter how remote a farm cottage, the Germans would go there sooner or later.

I had been able to avoid them so far mainly because of the nature of the ground. In order to visit a high-lying farm, soldiers would not walk up the glens and the hillsides where I had trudged. They would arrive in a car commandeered in a town or village where they had established their local Kommandantur. A car would give me adequate warning.

Now, though, I was entering lower lying ground with more numerous centres of habitation. I was likely to encounter the enemy at any time and in any place. To reach the English Army I should have to run the gauntlet of Hitler's forces where sheer population density would demand their heavier presence – in that narrow strip of territory lying between Clyde and Forth. What lay beyond I had only a vague idea. I did not know Southern Scotland at all, and to reach England should have to rely entirely on instinct and luck.

I turned away from Loch Katrine, branching off towards Loch Ard. This route, though, would take me into Aberfoyle, and that would not do at all. I chose a path to sweep well past the town to the south, beginning with a tramp through Loch Ard Forest. Where the forest ended, I found myself once again with a road to cross.

I was now past Aberfoyle, and had some idea of heading across towards the Campsie Fells. From these heights I hoped to be able to identify a route through the densely populated central belt.

For the past – how many days was it? – I had believed that I was exercising due caution, that I had been really canny in choosing my routes and in taking advantage of such cover as there was.

None of this had stopped my running straight into that paratrooper and failing even to suspect his presence.

Yesterday's brush with the aeroplane, too, was something that I ought to have anticipated. I should be on my toes listening for aircraft now. My early good luck had made me careless. I was becoming cocky. This was the way to run smack into German hands and pay the penalty. To do it very soon, too. I had seen ten men shot in retaliation. I had heard, though not seen, a man shot for not surrendering his shotguns. My own mother...

Let's face it. I had been damned lucky. Luckier, no doubt, than I deserved. All the way from Inverness to the fringe of Central Scotland, on foot, and still at large.

I still had the two SMGs, with a full magazine fitted to each. If I ran into trouble, I should be able to deal with it, but there was no point in going to look for it.

I withdrew into the trees. Probably no more than three hours until it would be fully dark.

I wasn't going to bed down for three hours. All too easy to nod off, and just as easy for someone to come tripping along and stumble over me. What I needed was a strong deciduous tree. The search took ten minutes, and I had the very thing.

Some people are natural tree climbers. I am not. All the same, I made it up the trunk, complete with SMGs. The angle of the branch was far from perfect, but it would do for a perch of no more than three hours. I sat with my back against the trunk, an SMG in my hand, and stretched both legs along the branch.

When leg cramps began to set in, I made myself put up with them for as long as I could bear. I told myself that I should not be able to move my legs, cross them, uncross them, dangle them or otherwise do anything likely to draw attention to myself when Germans could be down below. The earlier I began practising putting up with cramps and remaining immobile, the sooner I should be safe if trapped up a tree while woods were being searched. There was something I had ignored when taking provisions from my mother's store. Salt. I should need salt to fight against the cramps. An unopened box had faced me when I opened one of my mother's cupboards, and I had pushed it to one side as irrelevant. I knew better now.

I waited a clear hour before venturing to the edge of the trees. From now on, night was to be my companion. When nothing should move, I should move. Where there should be none but Germans, I should be.

There seemed a lot of cloud – about six tenths, I thought – but winds were moving it so as to obscure and reveal the moon at short intervals. Since there was no more than a half moon, the likelihood of my being exposed in open country by a sudden flood of light did not appear great.

I gave the land directly across the road a lengthy scrutiny. Unless I was mistaken, it was flat for miles – as far as the first slopes of the Campsie Fells. Scattered shrubs promised random concealment. Unless I were particularly careless, or unlucky, I ought to be well up on the Campsies before dawn. And learning to conceal myself.

Satisfied with having found a route to follow on the other side, I subjected the road itself to examination. In both directions all was quiet.

I took one of the SMGs into my hands, pulled back the bolt and loped across the carriageway. Ahead of me, the land stretched level all the way to Stirling. To my left, Scotland's only lake, the Lake of Menteith, lay hidden by trees.

After about a mile, I reached more woods, but did not enter them. In the darkness I had sufficient cover by walking along the edge of the trees.

What surprised me was the amount of noise I made simply by ambling at a comfortable pace. Clearly, each step made just the same sound in daylight, but until now I had remained unaware of my rustle and clatter. Only in darkness did the natural sounds of movement become clear to me – and what an obvious giveaway they would be to Gerry!

I made the ascent of the Campsie Fells in what struck me as very quick time indeed. The climbs of those last days had evidently made me stronger and suppler.

As I approached the summits, I became aware of a glow of light, similar to the first appearance of dawn, but with two factors that did not fit. The colour was too ruddy, and the radiance was in the wrong place: due south.

Once I attained the skyline, I saw the fire that was centred somewhere in Greater Glasgow.

A fire that covered a substantial area of the city. If I had to guess, I should estimate that no less than a square mile of buildings was being reduced to ashes.

How much damage was Scotland likely to suffer before the enemy was expelled?

Surely this fire was too big to be another act of sabotage by our own people, like the destruction of the aluminium works at Kinlochleven.

Had perhaps a resistance cell arisen and struck at the Germans right there in the city, and was this destruction the vengeance of the invader?

The thought of a resistance group was enticing. With my SMGs I could add firepower to any underground band.

The memory of my mother ended all such speculation. Did I want to be the cause of yet more hostage shootings? I should make a better contribution to driving out the invader by continuing with my resolve to join the English forces.

Meanwhile, I could do no more than pray that, whatever the German actions, there would be no gratuitous shootings as well.

I turned away and headed along the ridge of the Campsie range towards the Carron Valley Reservoir. This high-level artificial lake had been completed only within the last couple of years. I knew that it was well stocked with brown trout. I had matches. I could gather dry twigs. I could cook a trout.

My trout tickling was the almost classic example of beginner's luck. Tunic off and shirt sleeve rolled right up, I lay on the concrete bank of the reservoir with my bare arm dangling motionless in the water. With my other hand I held my flashlight low over the surface and shone a brief light.

Four trout came to investigate, one of them touching the fingers of my dangling hand. I had the fish out of there in double-quick time.

He was a fat one. I took him down the southern slopes below the reservoir and retreated into the very heart of the woods, where no light could be seen from outside. In orthodox Boy Scout style, I collected twigs for a fire, skewered the trout on a stripped stick and rigged up end supports for the spit.

Cooking took longer than I had anticipated. Only by rapid action was I able to keep feeding the fire and maintain the heat. The result was satisfying, if over-smokey. All the same, I was not foolish enough to delude myself that I should be able to live off the land like this. At some point I should have to show myself to a fellow countryman to buy food and other essential items. This was surely inevitable.

Meanwhile, I moved out on to open ground, dropping down the hillside towards High Banton. There was a smaller wood here, where I found the right tree to make myself comfortable. Day would not be long in coming, and I already had an idea of the route I should follow when that day came to an end.

13

IT occurs to me that I should explain just why I felt the need to keep out of the sight of my fellow countrymen as well as avoiding the Germans. It was simply that I knew too well the way that people let things slip, even – or perhaps sometimes especially – when they did not mean to.

The news that there was a uniformed Scots soldier in the district – and armed with German SMGs, no less – could never have been kept quiet, particularly if children had seen me. The manhunt that would have been unleashed – well, I scarcely need go into detail.

Had I been in civilian clothes, I could have moved about naturally, except of course for having to dodge the curfew. So why didn't I acquire civilian clothes? Why had I not changed into some of my own at my mother's house?

I was a soldier (still am) and fully intended to strike what blows at the enemy that I could. To do this legally – or at least to do it while retaining my self-respect – I needed to be in uniform. I had a weapon, and fully intended carrying it openly.

The idea of hiding my identity strikes me as the depth of cowardice. Should I come face to face with the enemy, I intended to confront him as a soldier.

I wear my uniform with pride, and if necessary I shall die in it as befits a soldier and the scion of soldiers. I shall not die from a German bullet or bullets while falsely attempting to represent myself as a civilian.

That next night turned chilly, but thankfully it was also moonless, and I was grateful to be able to force myself along at a brisk rate. The route I followed was as near to a straight line as any that I managed during my entire trek.

Avoiding roads of course, I passed between Kilsyth and Castlecary, marched on to Caldercruix, left Shotts on my left and finished up at the first sight of dawn in a wood a couple of miles east of Carluke.

I had crossed the entire north-south girth of the highly populated central belt and seen nothing of the occupying forces.

Could the worst be behind me? Naturally the worst was ahead. Reaching my objective was going to mean finding my way through the battle lines of two armies.

Meanwhile I should be unable to slacken my precautions.

Certainly my body was adapting well to tree-dwelling. My eyes, too, had rapidly become accustomed to my new life pattern.

For the coming day I found an almost perfect perch where two branches left their trunk almost like twins with only slight divergence. I was able to rest each leg at a comfortable angle and actually slept for most of the daylight hours.

When I woke in the early evening, I felt not the least hint of cramp.

There was one thing, though.

My kilt was a little slack and beginning to slip down at the hip.

The loss of weight was unsurprising. I had eaten nothing since that trout. I pulled in the kilt straps by one buckle hole.

Despite the weight loss and the empty stomach, I was feeling fit.

This was as well, since what faced me now were the Southern Uplands, where I did not know my way and where, on the approach to England, Germans were likely to be thicker on the ground.

How far had German forces penetrated into England? Or had they been thrust back onto our side of the border? What was certain was that the closer I drew to the Carlisle-Berwick line, the greater difficulty I should have in moving southwards at all. I was desperate to hear news, but naturally it would need to be the real thing, not German propaganda and distortion.

One thing in particular I had not heard. I did not doubt that it was posted up outside every building taken over as a Kommandantur, and elsewhere in the centres of cities, towns and villages. I had not heard it, and it certainly affected me, but truth to tell I did not want to hear it.

The subject I wished to avoid was what exactly had happened between the invaders and the Scottish Government. According to the one notice I had seen, a 'treaty of neutrality' had been concluded. I doubted if that was all. There could be no doubt that the NPS régime would have been forced to capitulate without conditions, to concede total German control over the country. This will have included an order that Scotland's armed forces were to disband, all weapons being handed over to the invader. The Edinburgh Government would have been compelled to issue an order to this effect.

This meant that I was now a rogue soldier no longer holding my government's commission, an illegal bearer of arms who under the laws of war could and would be shot as soon as captured.

Did this legal situation make nonsense of my attitude as outlined above, my determination to face the enemy as a soldier, not as a guerrilla? No, I say. My position was valid, since I had received no order to lay down my arms. If I had received such a command, would I have obeyed? I leave it to you. Like every other serviceman, I had sworn an oath to defend my country. That was what I was going to do. I am not going to argue the point.

Almost at once after I had set off with my now better-fitting kilt, I saw the dimmed lights of a truck on the road that ran across my path. Another. Then another. Altogether, a column of eight trucks was approaching.

I could see the silhouettes of soldiers sitting in rows in the back. Helmets were unmistakable, rifles stood upright. If all eight truckloads jumped down, spread out and began advancing in a search of the ground, I should be finished. Surely, though, they would not hunt for me in the dark?

The trucks did not stop. In the manner of old established country roads, their route turned a little this way and that, but the column kept on moving. It was following what looked to me like a route leading south and east towards the border.

I was in luck. Once those trucks had vanished, I waited quite a while without seeing any further lights or movements.

With no clear idea at all of which direction was the most suitable for my purpose, I struck south-east. I should not go due south, so much I did know. That would only bring me to the Carlisle area. I had to avoid large cities and any location that was likely to be a key centre of fighting.

Much as I was conscious of the need to keep my mind concentrated on searching the landscape, I could not stop myself wondering how the Germans had managed their invasion. With the Royal Navy controlling the North Sea, only paratroops could make that first critical landing. Not until the paratroops had established control could the mass of infantry be risked at sea. The whole operation launched from Norway, and a triumphant cooperative exercise of all the three services that constituted Hitler's Wehrmacht. With Norway in his hands, Hitler had no need for a risky Channel crossing.

I saw no more German transports that night. Nor did I cover such a distance as I had hoped. I lost some time in making a wide circle round Biggar. Anxious to make up for the delay, I came close to marching on into daylight. Dawn was already well on the way before I stopped in the cover of a wood on a decent sized hill. Here I had a burn, a principal requirement when camping out. This one provided excellent, clear drinking water.

Next night I faced hills as high as some of those I had tackled between Inverness and the Trossachs. I crossed one major road, without any idea of where I was. After that it was uphill again, and a good tramp across the heights until I came to a sizeable wood that had not only a burn running through it but boasted a small loch, too.

Hunger was now a constant companion. I thought that I might whisk a fish from the loch as I had tickled the Carron trout. That really had been beginner's luck. An absolute fluke. Here there were fish, but very few. All that I saw were small, and none ventured close to my hand.

Irritated by my failure, I did not climb a tree, but crawled into undergrowth and bedded down there. Tiredness from the night's exertions should have sent me into early sleep, but an empty stomach kept me awake. It kept my thoughts on food, too, and this did not help. I told myself that I ought to be able to trap a rabbit. Realistic planning and preparation of my food and water needs was long overdue.

I did not undertake it. I left my bed in the undergrowth some time around one a.m. and walked straight down the hillside towards a major road. Almost smack into the arms of a German patrol.

There were two of them, rifles slung over their shoulders, sauntering along the road in quiet conversation. I owed my life to their self-absorption rather than to my own speed of reaction.

They owed their lives to my unwillingness to inflict twenty casualties on the population of the district. Well before nearing the road, I had as usual drawn back the bolt of the SMG in my hands. The temptation simply to let fly at the two as they walked past me with heads down was fleeting, but powerful. The memory of a list of names that included my mother's seized my fingers with immobility. I could not inflict the same on even one other family.

I went into cover beside the road to watch the Germans wander on out of sight, then remained hidden for some minutes.

A half dozen paces took me across the road. On the far side flowed a river that I realized much later must have been the Tweed, Ahead, the route that I wanted to take was peppered with sharp contoured hills. I eased the bolt on the SMG into the safety position and began to follow the water downstream, taking care to remain out of sight of the road. I was keeping an eye on the hills, hoping to pick out the most favourable path between them.

I headed towards the nearest patch of woodland. With no idea of what lay ahead, I decided to keep on until reaching the end of the trees.

I had walked a little too long. Beyond the trees, open countryside already lay in early sunlight. No more than a quarter mile ahead, a low fence ran across the moorland, bobbing up and down with the undulations of the ground. For some seconds I simply stared, not knowing what to make of it.

Then it hit me. The border between Scotland and England! This was the fence symbolizing what the NPS had thought was such a superb idea for the future of the Scottish people. It was one of those ultra-sunny early mornings when every stone on the ground was illuminated in finest detail. Hanging around at the edge of the woods was asking for trouble.

I needed to go back in among the trees for a reasonable distance and find the right spot for bedding down. There was no shortage of climbable trees.

That border fence mesmerized me. Damn the thing! Whose confounded silly idea was separation in the first place? Who really thought that we could go it in the world alone? Look how 'independent' we were now. In trying to be friends with everybody, we had put our head into the lion's mouth.

Left and right I expected to see machine gun towers, but there was none. Of course. The Germans didn't need these. They were both sides of the border, and all of Britain was helpless,

One SMG was already in my hands. I pulled back the bolt and stepped straight out onto what I realized must be the moorland lower slopes of the Cheviots. I was going to cross that fence if it were the last thing that I did.

That it might indeed be the last thing did not occur to me while I was crossing the open ground. I was too fixated on reaching that wretched fence and walking through it into England.

All my pent-up anger – over that infantile referendum, the break-up of the British Union, the running down of Scotland to the status of unarmed easy prey, our self-degradation in abandoning England in her months of peril, the German invasion – all this righteous fury went into the last stride with which I flew up to the fence.

I seized the top of the structure with both hands, tore it down to the ground, went to the posts supporting it left and right, and forced these to lie on Britain's good soil. If only I could have ripped apart with such ease whatever surrender document the Edinburgh Government had signed with the German invader!

With considerable satisfaction, I carried my cocked SMG into England.

Now only one issue interested me: Where were the Germans? As you will realize, this was entirely the wrong question.

I should have been asking myself where I was going to hide for the remainder of this bright day.

Ahead and to my left was a large woodland. I made straight for it and in minutes was inside the trees. They were not what I needed. Firs, spruce, Scots pines – no perches among the branches here.

Against this, an advantage of a coniferous wood is that it offers an unlimited and most comfortable bed of needles. I picked a spot under a tree whose lowest branches practically brushed the earth.

Wherever the Germans were, they were nowhere near here. On the ground the day was as quiet as the sun was brilliant. Only on the ground. Far to the south, I could just – only just – detect the occasional sound of aircraft engines. Had the front moved already that far away?

Perhaps I could have marched on and met no enemy. It was better, though, to have as much rest as I could. Tonight I might run close to whatever fighting was taking place.

What German forces might be engaged? We had all seen film of the methods used in Poland, the Low Countries and France. Dive bombing and fast moving tank armies. Did the Germans have tanks here? And heavy artillery? Could they have brought in enough by sea?

In Scotland all that I had seen were paratroops and infantry, both without heavy weapons.

Could the invaders have pushed into England with light forces only? Unlikely. Yet according to the BBC they had pressed quite a way down the East Coast in the first days.

If they had advanced much farther, I had quite a trek still ahead of me – and my brogues were wearing noticeably thin. Noticeably in the literal sense that I could now feel any large or sharp edged stones through the soles.

I examined those soles. Not paper-thin yet, but card-thin. Once they had broken through at the critical point under the ball of the foot, I should be able to continue for a while with the aid of material laid inside the shoe. But for how long? And what material was I going to use as a liner?

It was out of the question that I could continue for many more days without showing myself at a farmhouse, or in a town or village. Ideally, I should venture into a village to buy boots or what are usually described as 'stout walking shoes'.

While I was at it, I should take advantage and buy food. Should I be in as much danger in the North of England as at home? What were the chances here of my being given away to German forces? I did not believe that any Englishman or woman would betray me intentionally to the enemy. As at home, it was the possibility of loose tongues that worried me. In particular, there was a danger from children chattering about what they had seen. I know how excited I should have been as a boy, had I spotted a figure like myself, wandering around armed in an embattled land, yet far from where I might be supposed to belong.

There seemed only one thing to do. I should enter a village after dark and hope that the local shoe shop owner – if there were a shoe shop – lived on the premises. I should knock him up. If I were lucky, he would not only have the tough footwear that I required, but would also be prepared to sell me some of the foodstuffs from his larder. This would save me having to knock up the local grocer, as well.

Where, in any case, was a village sizeable enough to meet my needs? I had no idea of my place in the landscape, and of course all road signs and place names in England and Wales had been taken down, so that they could not serve as aids to an invader. I should just have to follow a road - any road - and see where I finished up.

I waited until dusk and set off perhaps a little earlier than I should have. A couple of hours' tramp brought me to a railway line. Not a main line, but at least it was a railway, and it had to lead somewhere. If a train ran, here behind the German lines, I should be very surprised.

I stepped between the rails and took a pace forward onto a sleeper, landing on my heel. Then another pace, onto the next sleeper, again dropping onto my heel.

In this way I walked along that railway line for mile after mile, treading only on the heels of my brogues and preserving the soles for a little longer. My method of walking was tiring, yet had the advantage of forcing me to step out at a faster pace than was my usual.

In the course of the next hour, I passed through three tiny stations. They were nothing more than halts, and the few houses nearby were all in complete darkness. The English blackout, I realized, was going to be my best ally.

It was the darkest time of the night when I arrived at the outskirts of a moderately sized village. Would it be worth leaving the track to look for a shoe shop?

I doubted that the village was large enough to boast more than a post office/newsagent/general store. Plus at least two pubs, of course. Still, I could carry on with my heel-walking until the line led into a town, or at least into a larger village.

The station here was a substantial building with a high gable. To me, down below even the level of the platform, it appeared in the darkness overpoweringly huge.

'Right you are, Sunny Jim, just you stop right there'.

I could not see the source of the voice, and was in no position to react other than as ordered. I stopped.

14

'RIGHT. Let's have a look at you'. A torch shone into my face. 'Put those guns down. At once'.

The 'Sunny Jim' touch was reassuring. If the voice had been German, I should have tried a shot towards the torch.

I lowered both guns to the ground.

'Okay. Now come up here'.

I climbed onto the platform. The torch went out, and I could see the man holding it. I had abandoned my two SMGs at the order of an ordinary unarmed North of England policeman.

'Well, Jock', he asked, 'and where are you off to?'

'To join the English Army'.

'Taking your own guns with you?'

In five minutes we were like old friends. I explained about the paratroop drop at Fort George, about my journey so far, about how I acquired the SMGs, and finally about why I was walking along the railway sleepers.

Had I seen any Germans?

Not since I crossed into England.

'What about our boys?'

'If only I had!'

'No, we've not seen any, either, not since before the Gerries moved in. We can hear where they are, of course'.

There was less activity in the night, but still the odd aircraft drone and occasional faint thump of gunfire were unmistakable.

'Well, as you're not one of our boys but you're armed, I'm supposed to take you in. Pick up your guns. Let's get along'.

To where we were to get along, the constable did not specify. Nor did it matter. Important was that, 'taking me in' or not, he was happy to let me hold on to the SMGs.

At the police house, the officer led the way straight through to his living quarters. 'Well', he said as soon as he saw me under electric light, 'anyone can see you've been tramping for a week or two'. It was true. From head to foot I and my uniform were smeared with assorted quantities and varieties of earth.

Washing in hot water was a luxury that I had all but forgotten. Once I was cleaned up, I found myself sitting with a mug of strong tea in my hand and a hefty slice of pork pie on a plate beside me. I admit to being all but overwhelmed by a compulsion to go for that pie like the proverbial ravening wolf.

'Let's have a look at those shoes'.

I slipped off the brogues.

'You'll not go much farther in those, that's for sure. What's your size?'

The constable vanished. I made the pie all but disappear, too.

'Try these'. The constable was back, holding a pair of black boots.

I put down the mug of tea.

The boots were new. Police boots.

'Go ahead. Try them on'.

They certainly were my size. A bit stiff, but then, new footwear always is. I laced them, stood up and took a few steps back and forth. Being unused to boots, I was uncertain what to expect. With those first steps I realized at once the benefits of their support to ankles. For long distances, and particularly on slopes, brogues would never feel adequate again.

'All right?' The constable was looking at me with an expression half pleased, half enquiring.

'Very much all right'.

'Good. You'll get on better now. Those soles won't wear through in a hurry, but I must warn you: They'll take some breaking in. Don't try to do too much the first day or two. Keep your mileage down until you have broken them well in'.

'But aren't these your boots?'

We argued the toss for about ten minutes, or so it seemed. In the end, the constable agreed to accept the pound notes that I placed on his table. The boots, he assured me, were one of two spare pairs he had been keeping as future replacements.

'If you're moving only at night, you'd better stay here for today'.

These words were double edged. They were the most seductive I had heard since leaving the Fergusons in Glen Nevis, and of course I welcomed them. I also knew their danger. At all costs I must avoid becoming used to indoor comforts.

I had to keep going, I had to reach the English forces, and I had to fight the invader whatever the outcome for myself.

Scotland had to be liberated, but first the invader needed to be chased from English soil, where he was threatening to take a stranglehold similar to the one he had effected with such ease in my misguided homeland.

Night was almost finished. The constable went upstairs to warn his waking wife of my presence. A smiling, bustling soul, she came down in haste and sped into the kitchen.

I need not dwell on the hot bacon, the buttered toast and the rest of it. England, on a war footing, had food rationing. I had the strongest suspicion that the constable and his wife had sacrificed their week's allocation of bacon for their visitor, not to mention their butter. Of course they denied this, and with the food already cooked and placed before me, I could not refuse it. Not until I was on my way that night did it occur to me to wonder how food distribution could possibly function in the rear of the German lines and in a battle area generally. The explanation lay no doubt in the advantages of living in farming country, with the occasional availability of supplementary foodstuffs.

Most of that day I rested on the policeman's couch, needing only once to make a call on my reserves of vigour. This was necessary to resist offers of a hefty meal at midday.

Newspapers were not reaching this part of the country, but we could at least receive the BBC news broadcasts. From them I learned that the scene of fiercest fighting was in and around 'an important city in the North-East'.

Meanwhile, the Luftwaffe was maintaining its attacks on Channel ports (not specified). These raids maintained in English minds the fear of a cross-Channel invasion, tying no doubt the bulk of their forces in the Home Counties and all along the South Coast.

'Strictly speaking, I ought to take those off you for the Home Guard', said the constable, eyeing my two SMGs. 'This is a country at war, we are fighting off an invasion and you are a foreigner bearing military arms. I ought to lock you up'. Of course he was right. 'I'm only letting you keep them because you're heading straight for the bastards and you obviously know what you're doing'.

I hoped that he was right. I had explained how I acquired the guns, but those incidents did not make me a battle-hardened veteran.

'Here'. I handed him one of the weapons. It was fair payment for his turning a blind eye to the other. 'The magazine', I told him, 'is full'. After emptying one at that Fieseler, I still had a full magazine in each. The man was delighted, but no more so than I with the brand new boots.

Stronger than I had felt since that first day of the invasion, I set off soon after dark to the constable's admonition: 'Mind what I told you, now. Don't try and go too far tonight. Take it easy and wait until those boots are well and truly broken in. You'll cripple yourself if you don't. Patience now will pay dividends later on'.

These were wise words, and I resolved to abide by the instruction they contained.

With these boots, I had no need now to walk along the railway track. Nonetheless, the constable told me where it would lead, and to follow its route suited my ideas exactly.

Shortly beyond the village, the line turned due south. This was perfect.

Twelve miles or so were all that I covered or felt like walking. I stopped where the railway line crossed Hadrian's Wall. Not that there was much of the wall to be seen. A short fragment, and a sign pointing the way to a fort. Someone had not thought this one worth taking down.

The ground was flat here, and there was a river. I found cover. Not very good cover, but it offered sufficient concealment if no one pried too closely.

The sounds of battle were close now, perhaps no more than twenty miles. Most important was that I had so far neither run into Germans nor seen any sign of them. Another night's trek, and I should surely encounter some English unit to which I could attach myself.

I had a short sleep, and set off south in daylight.

15

AN hour brought me, after crossing the Tyne, to Hexham. The first people whom I passed took no notice of me, not even of the SMG on my shoulder. Presumably they could not recognize that this was a German weapon being carried into their midst.

'About time, Jock!' were the first words addressed to me. They came from an elderly, grey-haired gent who paused to lean on his stick.

'You can say that again', I told him.

'I was with your lot in the last do', he said. 'Attached to 51st Highland Division. Magnificent boys, couldn't have wished for better. They knew how to deal with Gerry, all right. Impossible to believe you wouldn't come in, this time'.

'If the Army had been asked, we should have'.

A lady hanging on to the hand of a small boy looked at me in astonishment. 'You're a long way from home, aren't you?'

'I don't think so', I told her. 'I'm in Britain. This is my home'.

'Hear, hear!' Some clapping came from behind me.

I turned. A half dozen people had stopped. They had questions.

'Do you know how far away the Gerries are?'

'Where are our boys? We haven't seen any'.

'Is Scotland sending troops at last?'

'Why haven't you been here before this?'

That one at least I could answer. 'It wasn't my choice. If it had been left to me, we should have been here from the beginning'.

'Better late than never, Jock, but why on earth did Scotland break away in the first place?'

'Search me. I was certainly never in favour of separation, but was too young to vote at the time. Even if I had voted against, it wouldn't have made any difference. Some kind of collective madness seemed to have gripped the people'.

'It was those smart-aleck NPS chaps with their propaganda', put in an elderly bald-headed fellow. 'Everything was going to be better because the Scots could do everything better. Enough to turn anyone's head. And all the while they had their eyes on the taxes from the whisky'.

'And much good it has done them'. This from a young, studious looking chap who must just have been reaching the age for call-up. 'Couldn't people see what was likely to happen?'

'People always see what they want to see, and blind themselves to whatever they don't want to see', I told him. 'Whether we had gone independent fifty years ago, or weren't to do it for another fifty years from now, it would be the same. Wishful thinking all along the way. And the thing not thought through properly'.

'Where are you off to, anyway?' the woman with the little boy wanted to know.

'He's going to join our boys, aren't you?' This from the man with the stick who had first accosted me.

'You bet. If I can get past the German forces'.

'Let's hope you do. We're just waiting for them to arrive'.

The tranquil spirit of these ordinary people, 'just waiting' for their invaders to arrive, was amazing.

'He's brought his own gun with him', someone pointed out.

This produced a small cheer. It was beginning to be embarrassing.

'Well, I'd better get on my way. I'm only sorry to be arriving late'.

I turned away to claps on the shoulder and cries of 'Good luck, Jock'.

Without risking breaking into a run, I hurried on through the town as fast as was seemly. Though it has an impressive abbey, Hexham is not large. I was back out into the countryside in perhaps ten minutes. By this time it was almost dark.

Under wartime conditions, no maps were available for sale in England. It was another measure akin to the dismantling of road signs. I had no idea where the road I was on would lead me. All that mattered was that it ran generally towards the south.

From the east came the unmistakable sounds of battle. Were the English chasing the invaders back?

What the hell! I made my decision right there and then. I had gone far enough south. I turned to the east, headed towards the gunfire, desultory now. Nothing more than medium artillery, I thought.

Some hours' determined march until it was dark, and as I crested a rise I saw for the first time flashes over the horizon.

The lights of battle.

There was nothing here that one could really call a hill. These were the natural undulations of a landscape edging unhurriedly into a river valley.

Here the flares of battle were brighter, the rattles and crashes more distinct.

Firing nearby.

More firing, even closer.

I went flat onto the ground. Could see nothing. Tried to understand what I was hearing.

Vehicles now. A lot of them. Coming up from behind.

Someone was moving a large body of forces through the night. Before I could see any vehicles, let alone identify them, a large scale fire fight erupted round me. Flashes were cutting into the darkness, lighting terrain, illuminating for an instant a man and a weapon, revealing the protagonists who were meeting in violent encounter.

I was in the middle, between the English and their invaders.

No, I wasn't.

I was surrounded by Germans.

One thing this war had taught us already. The Germans were incredibly fast movers. They raced on to wherever their strategic objectives lay, not bothering about the regions and towns that they bypassed.

Not until the whole territory lay at their feet, and there was no more fighting to be done, did they set about systematic occupation of the whole land. We had seen it in Poland, we had seen it in France. On the cinema newsreels, that is. Now the English were seeing it at first hand.

Towns like Hexham had no priority among Germany's military aims. For the moment their people were interested bystanders. Heaven help them if the Germans should achieve their overall purpose.

If the invaders were stopping to make a fight of it here, wherever I was, then here was on their list of objectives. It was easy to see why.

'An important city in the North-East'. Newcastle was not just a seaport capable of handling massive quantities of cargo. It was also where the bulk of England's tanks were built. The mass of vehicles I had heard were surely bringing English forces to prevent their main tank factory falling into German hands.

The Germans who were all round me must have pursued the coastal route as the BBC had reported, and had now swung inland to surround the Newcastle conurbation, doubtless to pop up on the southern side of the city.

That had been a favourite trick of Frederick the Great's, hadn't it? He would make a frontal assault and then, while the enemy was fully engaged facing him, he would send forces round to his rear. Napoleon had used that trick, too.

Were Hitler's generals schooled in the same technique? It must have been in the course of some such manoeuvre that their troops had engulfed me.

Shells were landing none too far away.

For an instant they lit up Germans, individuals and small groups, moving across the ground, crouching, crawling, running.

Finger on the trigger of my SMG, I waited for the next detonation. When it came, the flash showed me two Germans, crouching together.

I fired a short burst in their direction, without being able to see any result.

A second shell gave me a single target. So did a third.

I had fired three bursts at four Germans, not knowing whether I had hit any. My magazine could well now have only one round left, but I waited nonetheless for a fourth opportunity.

Whether what hit me were fragments from a shell or from a grenade, I never knew. My leg felt as though it had exploded, and I lost consciousness.

16

'YOU can have him now, Captain'. The MO let go of my wrist and stepped back. A severe looking young captain with a fair thin moustache, possibly a year or two younger than myself, took his place. The insignia of the Military Police struck a surprising note.

'You have a lot of questions to answer. The sooner we get them over with, the better for you'.

I was in an English military hospital, but where this was I did not know. My leg felt numb, it was plastered and lay outside the blankets. I had recovered consciousness while being loaded into a field ambulance by a couple of RAMC privates. There were multiple fractures to my leg, and I was driven a long way. Now here I was in a private room. Frankly, I should have preferred being in an open ward along with English wounded.

'I have plenty of questions, too', I told the captain. 'Have you kept the Gerries out of Newcastle?'

'That'll be enough of that', the captain snapped. 'We want to know what you were doing in the uniform of a neutral country' – I should not have thought it possible to pour into the word neutral so much contempt as the captain managed – 'and armed with enemy weaponry'.

For some seconds I was mute.

Only then did I notice the sergeant sitting silent in the corner with shorthand notebook and poised pencil.

I gave the captain my name, rank and number, started to explain how I had left Fort George when the Germans landed. The captain cut me short. 'You can drop that nonsense right now. You were with a German unit, using German weapons. It's just your bad luck that you weren't killed outright instead of nearly losing a leg'.

The penny dropped. Why, the bloody fools! I laughed in the captain's face. He did not like it.

Our exchanges from then on could very easily have developed into a shouting match. I declined to drop to the level of the captain's hostility, or to honour his absurd insinuations by countering them.

I told my story truthfully and left it at that. About seeing the workmen shot at Fort William, about seeing the aluminium smelter sabotaged at Kinlochleven, about killing the paratrooper and taking his SMG, about bringing down a Fieseler Storch into Loch Katrine, about finding out that my mother had been shot as a hostage. All that I omitted was the killing of the second paratrooper and the acquisition of another SMG. Plus where I had left the weapon.

I had no wish to cause any trouble for the policeman who had been so generous and helpful to me.

For the next three days I saw no one but hospital personnel. I did not know it, but learned later that a soldier had been sitting the entire time on guard outside the door of my room, a loaded weapon cradled in his lap. I was not so much a patient as a prisoner, and a suspect one at that.

On the fourth day I had a visit from a major. Not Military Police, but an amiable red-faced giant from an infantry regiment.

His first words put everything straight.

'May I first offer my sincerest condolences on the death of your mother'.

I sat up, looked at him, saw the genuine sympathy in his eyes. 'You've had it confirmed?'

'Oh yes. You'd be surprised how many people we have working for us in Scotland. We've had the lists of all the hostages shot, from the beginning. As for the rest' – the major gave me a curious look – 'it looks as though you have been rather modest. We've heard about two paratroopers being killed in the area you mentioned'.

I said nothing.

'And the interesting thing is', the major went on, 'there were no hostages shot there'.

I flopped back into the pillows and released a deep sigh. I had been carrying guilt with me every step of the way from Taynuilt. It was a burden that I feared I should never shed.

Thank goodness for a decent German commander!

'You say', said the major, 'that you want to join an English regiment'.

'I walked from Inverness to Newcastle to do just that – and not by the shortest route, either'.

'Well, your credentials are fine'.

'You've checked my service record?'

'Not just that. Of course we know it all, from Sandhurst on. But as I said, we've good sources in Scotland. The first paratrooper was definitely killed by a sgian dubh. An expert was called in by the Germans and confirmed it'.

'They didn't think it could have been just anyone carrying a sgian dubh?'

'It might have been. But then there was the second chap who "delivered" your missive. He was killed with German ammunition from a German weapon. Like the one you had with you. It made everything credible'.

Again I said nothing.

The major smiled. 'Why you should be coy about that one, I really can't imagine. Still, it's your business, and I'm sure you know what you are doing'.

I did. As I have said, I was anxious to protect my friendly policeman.

The major leaned forward to shake my hand. 'As soon as your leg is fit enough we'll see about signing you up. And getting you a temporary wartime commission. Don't see any great difficulty, especially in view of your past'.

That wasn't important to me. I just wanted to be able to get at the Gerries.

What the major meant was that I had already, in my Sandhurst days, sworn an oath 'to be faithful and bear true allegiance to His Majesty King George the Fifth, his heirs and successors'.

I should renew that vow happily now, should it be required of me.

Meanwhile, my leg needed first to heal sufficiently to satisfy an Army MO.

It took six weeks.

The surgeon who stuck all the broken pieces back together told me that it would be a three-month job.

I wasn't having that, and told him that I should halve the time. Of course, he pooh-poohed this, pointing out that natural physiological processes could not be hurried.

'Don't you know', I asked him, 'that there's a war on?'

In the end, this was the argument that counted. England was so short of subalterns – indeed, of every kind of serviceman and woman – that blind eyes had to be turned in all kinds of cases.

Subalterns were perpetually in short supply because their life expectancy at the front was so brief. No matter how short mine should be, I was going to take plenty of the other side with me, I was sure of that.

Meanwhile, leg up and immobile, I have been spending my days and evenings typing out this record of my adventures, such as they have been, from the moment that General Kurt Student's paratroops arrived over Fort George. A chap from the Ministry of Information, along with a senior officer in the English Army, turned up one day to ask me to do this. The idea is, I gather, to publish my account as part of a campaign to let people in the outside world know what difficulties England is in without the partner on whom she had been able to rely since 1707.

I gather that my narrative is expected particularly to stir the Americans. England needs materials from America, and if my story helps to convince Americans of England's merits and deserts, I shall feel less embarrassed about writing so much about myself.

I must say that staff at the English military hospital have been marvellous. They have had my blood- and earth-stained kilt and tunic cleaned, and found from somewhere a pair of socks (mine are shrapnel casualties) and some officer's brogues. The brogues have turned out to be a half size too big, but insoles have cured that. In any case, this kind gesture was only to make me feel better once I was able to leave bed and do some testing of my mended leg. It was wonderful to be able to hobble in the grounds in my regimental gear, but the whole thing has been, like the fresh commission that I expect, no more than a temporary expedient. Soon I shall be kitted out in the battledress uniform of an English infantry regiment. It is a case of 'any day now' for the final medical examination that will approve my entry into the English war machine.

I did not myself hear the news on the wireless. An orderly who came in with a cup of tea on a tray told me of it in some excitement. The Germans had already occupied Carlisle and were fighting for total control of Newcastle. Now they brought ashore a fresh army just south of Middlesbrough, while Student's airborne forces landed on the opposite coast, at Morecambe Bay. Both landings were preceded and supported by aerial bombardment, chiefly through Junkers 88 machines operating from Turnhouse, outside Edinburgh.

In overall command of this operation is General Erich von Manstein, who quickly sealed off Middlesbrough from the south. Lieutenant-General Erwin Rommel, a little-known commander, meanwhile raced with mobile forces deep inland. Rommel moved at an alarming pace, bypassing Darlington and storming on towards the Yorkshire Dales.

Having consolidated their Lancashire beachhead, based around Carnforth, Student's men soon received reinforce- ments and headed northeast in an obvious move to link up with Rommel. This manoeuvre, if successful, will cut off all those English forces who have rushed northwards to fight off the invasion from Scotland. What this will mean for England's overall strength does not bear contemplation.

From the outset, the RAF has been in action against these latest German arrivals. With Junkers machines flying non-stop shuttle attacks from Turnhouse, a bitter struggle has developed for aerial mastery over the battlefield. Meanwhile, in an effort to divide RAF resources, French-based Luftwaffe squadrons are persisting in almost round-the-clock bombing of targets in the English south – London and the Channel ports. At a stroke, England has been placed in imminent danger of military collapse.

What this situation has demonstrated beyond dispute is Scotland's inestimable value to an enemy as an advanced base for operations against England. Thanks to the NPS government's 'neutrality' and inactivity, the Germans have been able to transfer great numbers of troops and aircraft to Scotland from Norway. Not, though, without loss. Despite losing a number of vessels to Admiral Dönitz's U-boats, the Royal Navy has sunk several German transports in the North Sea.

There is no need to dwell on the shame of Scotland's refusal to support England's fight. It has become more than adequately clear that by her nonsensical break away from the Union Scotland made herself weaker and appallingly vulnerable. In practice, too, she has made herself a passive ally and accomplice in Hitler's war.

Can anyone doubt that the Führer would never have dared to send in troops to invade any part of a Britain that was still united? Of course, I admit that one can never prove this point, one way or the other. We cannot possibly replay that perilous period after the fall of France.

I hope, nonetheless, that we have all now learned our lessons: that self-centred nationalism can rebound in ghastly fashion; that by placing one's own interests first and refusing to help others, one can find oneself deservedly without friends or assistance when one's own circumstances go wrong; that troubles can be better countered through unity with those with whom one enjoys a common language, a shared culture and centuries of joint experiences and history. We should also never forget that the unexpected lurks always round the corner. Without allies, England faces the most appalling uphill fight to defeat the invader. I am happy to record that many thousand Scots are now in her ranks. To a man, these are determined not just to destroy Hitler's forces, but equally to expunge the shame of the nationalists' self-centred abandonment of our neighbours.

A military hospital somewhere in England, summer 1941

EPILOGUE

WHAT you have read so far is a personal experience of those momentous days in 1940 and 1941, when England, alone and invaded, found herself on the brink of collapse. No one at that point knew what stood before us. We knew only that if England collapsed it was going to be grim. We needed a miracle.

And we had one.

It was inevitable that Hitler and Stalin should come to blows over Poland. Inevitable, too, that Stalin should take advantage of Hitler's commitment of almost all of his forces to the bitter Battle for Britain.

Stalin used the excuse of some petty boundary uncertainties to launch armies westwards towards the River Oder. Others pushed northwards along either bank of the Vistula, towards Danzig. The Soviet forces joined up to cut off East Prussia from the main body of the Reich. These moves were followed by the Soviet invasion of Romania and occupation of the Ploesti oilfields.

With only a minimum of forces on the ground in Poland, the Führer had no choice.

When France was on the verge of collapse, French forces were withdrawn from Norway to defend their homeland. Now German forces had to be withdrawn from Britain to fight off the Soviet invader.

Hitler's order to withdraw came with a renewal of his 'final appeal to reason' – the peace overture to London that he had made after the collapse of France.

Churchill's flat rejection was broadcast worldwide. England would continue to wage war on Germany until 'the scourge of Hitler' was 'lifted from the brows of mankind'.

English forces saw to it that the evacuation of Germans from British soil was a costly undertaking.

The Royal Navy had not sustained the level of losses borne by the RAF, and was able to blockade the North Sea route to Germany far better than it had in the early days of the German invasion.

In the face of persistent Luftwaffe attacks and Admiral Dönitz's U-boats, Royal Navy ships patrolled Britain's East Coast and darted up and down the Channel, waiting for German transports. One after another, a good proportion of these went to the bottom.

Evacuating his troops from Britain was a more costly exercise for Hitler than the invasion had been.

As soon as the last of the Germans had quit British soil – many to die at sea – we were given leave. I set off at once for my late mother's home near Oban. It had suffered from being unoccupied, but there was no damage that could not be repaired once we were finished with this war.

I had been hoping to lay my hands on Major Gehring, Commandant of Oban District, who had ordered the shooting of my mother and nineteen other hostages.

I had no chance of catching him. The Germans left Scotland first, in good order and with amazing speed. One day, so I was told, they were still there; on the next they were gone.

The Scottish Government, promising a fresh election after the war, reassembled at Holyrood. In the face of public pressure, it capitulated at once and introduced conscription.

I stayed with my English unit.

Hitler's next move looked like suicide.

After the Japanese attack on Pearl Harbor, he followed Japan's lead and declared war on the United States. Bringing in America's industrial production and reserves of manpower against Germany did indeed prove to be suicidal. The consequence was that England, having faced Hitler alone for a full year, now found herself in a life-saving alliance with America and the Soviet Union.

Another twelve months saw the Red Army mastering the German forces and beginning the long turn-round of fortunes that was to end with the downfall of the Reich.

When the time came to invade Normandy together with the Americans, in 1944, I naturally hoped to be part of the show. Instead, I spent those exciting days as an instructor, passing on to young men with temporary wartime commissions, like myself, most of what I had learned at Sandhurst thirteen or fourteen years earlier. For me, victory was an anti-climax. My military career ended, as the poet says, not with a bang but with a whimper.

Now that Hitler is defeated and his hideous apparatus of dictatorship dismantled, we may well think that there can be no further dangers to threaten us.

I should not recommend such complacency.

What I should recommend is for Scotland immediately and irrevocably to reunite with her fellow Britons. For her own, and for her neighbours' good.

And for goodness' sake never even to contemplate such a self-destructive idea again.

VII

UNKIND of me, perhaps, but I could not help comparing the poor doctor's propagandistic literary efforts with those of Otto and Elise Hampel, a Berlin couple who during the Second World War wrote and distributed a few hundred postcards calling on Germans to rise, throw out Hitler and end the fighting.

This well-meant resistance campaign had no effect whatever. Almost all of the pair's laboriously written and carefully distributed cards were immediately handed in to the Gestapo by the loyal citizens who found them. Tracked down by a relentless police machine, the Hampels were executed for high treason. The couple had been unbelievably naïve in misinterpreting their fellow-citizens' values. The same, I thought, ought not to prove true of poor Dr Bruce. Like the Hampels, the young registrar was given no chance of influencing anybody. And like the Hampels, the doctor too finished up dead. Why did that have to happen?

Long after the Hampels, in Cold War Berlin, I had witnessed the futile efforts – and lost lives – of so many would-be world-changers. Almost without exception these idealists were harmless. All the same, innocuous or not, on the far side of the Wall they could still be consigned to the executioner.

Is this what had happened to the young doctor? No. I could not believe that anyone had killed him because of his stance against independence. Political murders did not happen in Britain. We did not settle our differences with bullets. We argued them out with words and reason.

Yet it was the very existence of *The Lion's Mouth* that convinced me Dr Bruce had not committed suicide. At the time of his death his typescript was with the Edinburgh publisher. He had no idea then that his effort was going to be turned down, and had presumably been living in a rosy glow of expectation. The doctor would not have stepped in front of a train.

For a certainty, he had been murdered. Not, though, because of *The Lion's Mouth*. Whoever killed Dr Bruce had stolen no valuables from the body, was interested only in papers that the doctor had been desperate to protect. Another copy of the doctor's literary efforts?

Why should he feel that he needed to secure this in a wrist chain briefcase? Surely, even the self-delusional expectations of the first time author did not extend that far. Something quite different, then, in the briefcase. What was worth killing for and worth locking away? Money, usually. Mr Hill-Forrester was adamant that they were not handwritten papers that he had seen going into the case. Papers with a specific monetary value, perhaps. Like bearer bonds. That would be a self-evident theory, but I was disinclined to grasp the obvious.

Dr Bruce's life was going to require some exploration. No interests beyond his work and his fiancée? Now that I had read *The Lion's Mouth* I realized that there was certainly more to the young registrar than that.

If what Grant had told Dr Bruce was not fiction, there could well have been something sinister in the dying man's involvements. Unless, of course, Grant was a story-teller whose head injuries had robbed him of the capacity to distinguish between reality and the products of his own imagination. Like an actor who might begin to believe that he really is the character whom he portrays.

My first thought was that we should hand Dr Bruce's typescript over to the police. No. It was the dead man's property and should go to his parents. Nothing, of course, to stop me making a copy for the police. Yet what did the work prove? No more than that Dr Bruce had been a young man desperate not to see Scotland torn from the United Kingdom. Probably half of the population felt like that, and no one was going to set about a programme of mass slaughter to ensure a vote for independence. Unless I could find some meaning in the dying Grant's remarks, and a connection in them to Dr Bruce's death, the whole thing looked to me like a mare's nest. All the same, I could not simply put it out of my mind.

Among Scotland's police I had one, and only one, friend who might assist in some clandestine research.

We had an operative once who went missing in the North of England. He was a formerly dedicated German Communist whom I had turned and brought across from just outside East Berlin. Strictly speaking, his disappearance was none of my affair. My job was at Berlin Station. Yet because the man had been one of my protégés, they brought me across just the same, and called in Special Branch as well.

Our chap turned up all right in the end, and no harm was done. During the search, one thing had led to another, and via Special Branch I came to know a senior Scots policeman to whom I shall refer as Nick. Since those days, Nick had climbed to the level of a Deputy Chief Constable. Before turning to Nick now, I re-read the newspaper reports of Dr Bruce's death.

I remembered how the young registrar had helped me on one occasion, when the iron collar that was to keep my neck rigid sprang apart. As I have said, I found the man delightful and, like Mr Hill-Forrester, could not imagine that he had ever entertained any thought of suicide.

Of course I had known suicides. Two of my people in East Germany, and one in Czechoslovakia, had managed to kill themselves just as they were due to be picked up by their own republics' security services. By so doing, they had ensured that they could not be tortured into giving away anyone else. These were practical suicides, having nothing to do with the individual's state of mind.

Nick and I had remained in loose contact over the years by means of Christmas cards, though we had not seen each other since our missing man was located. I telephoned to make an appointment. The hand that gripped mine next morning displayed unstinting warmth.

By Jove, though, Nick had lost a lot of hair. I remembered him with a healthy black mop, and now there was covering only to left and right. He had put on weight, as well. Still, so had I. It was only the spell in hospital that had let me lose a lot of flab. I had no cause to feel smug about anyone else's rounded-out abdomen.

Whatever else, Nick's light blue eyes were still sincere, and his smile was as warm as ever.

'Missing Berlin, Ian?'

I was, but only when I thought about it. Berlin had long been my second home – and I should be ungrateful not to think of her with affection. All the same, I was happy to be living out the rest of my life in my homeland. 'What about you, Nick? Not much farther for you to climb, is there?'

'Not looking for it, Ian. Expecting to retire in not much more than another year'.

'And then? Not planning to go and live in Spain by any chance, are you?'

'Good lord, no. Whatever gave you that idea?'

'It's just that I keep hearing of people who are doing that sort of thing, taking their pensions to live abroad. I don't understand it. I could never turn my back on my own country'.

'As it happens, Ian, we are looking for a house in your part of the world'.

'In Argyll?'

'Or perhaps in Wester Ross. We haven't decided yet'.

We cut the personal talk, and I came out with my request. I needed to examine all the papers concerning the death of Dr Bruce. I stressed 'all'.

'If', I suggested, 'you can tell me anything about any Polish criminals who might have made enemies here, that will be a big help'.

'Poles? Sort of Polish mafia, do you mean?'

'Might be something like that. Could be just one or two individuals'.

'I can tell you this, Ian. I know of no organized Polish crime. What Poles get up to is more like disorganized crime'. Nick laughed, and I remembered how he would entertain a tableful of us while we were searching for my missing man. 'What are you expecting? Some sort of a gang war between Scots and Polish crooks?'

'Frankly, Nick, I've no idea. It's just a possibility I've thought of'.

'Well, are there any particular names you have in mind?'

'Don't know yet. Just a hint about Poles in general, that's all'.

'Okay, Ian. Give me the word once you have something definite that I can go on. Come in tomorrow morning at nine o'clock, and the files on that dead doctor will be ready for you. You can use the empty office next to mine. One condition. You can spend as long as you like looking at things here, but nothing must be taken from these premises. Understood?'

'Understood'.

The file was certainly a hefty one. If I had supposed that the investigation had been skimped or that the police had rushed to a conclusion, I was wrong. No Poles had been interviewed or even mentioned, but there were records of the questionings of Mr Hill-Forrester and of a half dozen more of Dr Bruce's hospital colleagues, interviews with his parents, his fiancée Janine, her parents and a handful of the doctor's friends. Among all of these, rejection of suicide was unanimous and emphatic. Well, I said to myself, it would be, wouldn't it?

No one could have any idea of what was going on in Dr Bruce's mind. At that stage, of course, not knowing whether Simon Grant's dying ramblings meant anything or were fantasy, I myself had to keep an open mind. Yet whether it had been suicide or murder, Dr Bruce's death could well have been connected with those missing papers. Since someone else had been anxious to get his hands on them, surely these had to be the key. The doctor had got himself mixed up in something or other – nasty, as he had said. The notes he had made of Simon Grant's ramblings had made him the man who knew too much. I had to find both Grant's accomplices and the mysterious Poles.

Where did I begin? I began with a visit to the location of the poor man's death, just outside Craigendoran station. Dr Bruce had left his train there late at night to visit his fiancée and her parents on the outskirts of Helensburgh. Several hours later he was sliced into fragments by the Mallaig to Glasgow fish train. If it was a fish train. Once, that is unquestionably what it would have been. These days, thanks a million to the EU, there is as good as no significant fishing done from what were once the busiest of our harbours. All that I can say for certain is that whatever the fatal train was carrying, it was not people. It passed over the body at 3.44a.m., some hours before the first passenger train was due to move on that route.

Dr Bruce was alive when the train hit him. If the suicide theory were correct, he must have spent more than four hours hovering around Craigendoran station, waiting for the next train. Not a thing that I should like

153

to spend my time doing. Nothing there but open tracks and a platform. Four hours kicking one's heels – and avoiding being seen.

Possible, of course, but what made both suicide and accident unlikely to me was the removal of the papers from his briefcase. A thief robbing the body would not have taken papers and left the doctor's wallet. Nor would he have left his watch, which miraculously had been just missed by the train wheels. Plunder of the papers made it look as though this had been a straightforward murder with a specific object. The question was whether the victim had been rendered unconscious before being pushed or laid onto the tracks.

The main part of his briefcase had remained attached to Dr Bruce's wrist. After the papers were removed, the case had been relocked and the key returned to one of the owner's pockets. This could mean only one thing: an attempt to suggest that the doctor had been carrying an empty case. Whatever the papers were, the murderer had tried to direct attention away from them. And whatever they had been, the doctor had no copies of them at home. Nor had any been found at his hospital accommodation. Otherwise, Mr Hill-Forrester would surely have said so.

Though a key to his briefcase was found in Dr Bruce's pockets, there was none with him for the wrist chain. He had kept one at his home and another with his fiancée Janine. Presumably he had needed a third in his accommodation at the hospital. Yet none had surfaced among his property there. Nor did he have one on him. Not a man for taking risks on journeys, our Dr Bruce.

VIII

THE Deputy Chief Constable, Nick, was unsurprised at the lack of results from my visits to Dr Bruce's parents and to his fiancée. He had not expected me to produce anything fresh. On the other hand, the two keys animated him. Of course they fitted the wrist chain, and he was annoyed that once the shattered briefcase had been detached from the body his men had not seen any necessity of looking for keys.

For two days at police headquarters I remained immersed in the official records of the likeable registrar's death. I could find nothing to prove beyond question that his death could not have been either suicide or accident.

'Any of these boys look interesting, Ian?' Nick pushed a dozen files onto the desk where I was working. The photograph of a Pole decorated each dossier. Eleven men, one young blonde woman. None, of course, meant anything to me. Not even the crimes listed were of any interest.

'This chap looks like a bit of a recidivist', said Nick, indicating the photograph of a fellow in his mid-twenties whose prolifically bulging face suggested the absurd notion of a pregnant walnut. 'Three times we've pulled him in now, but as you can see, nothing worth more than six months'.

I looked at the name – K.B. Buta – and the details in the file. It was going to take me time to go through this lot.

'Bear with me', I asked.

'That sounds like the motto of a nudist club'. Yes, still the same full-of-fun Nick.

I combed all the files. Nothing pointing to any serious threat to the Queen's peace, nor suggesting sufficient systematic or repeated criminality to antagonize Grant and his devotees. Wasting my time here. No point imposing any further on Nick's courtesy. My work at police headquarters was finished. I invited Nick and his wife to my home for the coming weekend. We parted with mutual assertions of how much we looked forward to this further meeting, and I promised a particularly fine Campbeltown malt.

'Thank you, sir', Nick protested. 'I never drink when off-duty'. Squeezing rather than shaking my hand, he added: 'Sorry for the poor doctor, of course, but I'm damned grateful that all this has brought us back together. We must never lose touch again – and once I am retired we blessed well shan't. I'll see to that'.

I could not have asked for greater helpfulness, yet had not found the least particle of evidence to substantiate my conviction that Dr Bruce had been murdered. That, I reflected on the drive back to Argyll, was the trouble. All I had was a conviction, nothing more. Just a feeling.

I halted at my gates and leaped out to open them. The sound was unmistakeable. Inside the house my telephone was ringing. Without pausing to reach inside the Jaguar and switch off the engine, I fumbled the house key from my pocket and raced indoors.

'Mr Greig?' The voice could not be mistaken. Dr Bruce's father.

'Oh, Mr Greig, two men were here just now, asking for you. I gave them your phone number. I hope that is all right'.

'Oh yes, perfectly OK'.

'The only thing was, they seemed curious to know where you lived. Wanted to know if the dialling code meant that you lived in Oban. I told them no, but I'm afraid that I gave them a rough idea, as much as I know. I'm sorry. It was only after they'd gone that it occurred to me...'

'That's all right. Just one thing. Did they sound like Poles, by any chance?'

'Poles? No. They were two Scotsmen'.

'Well, thank you very much for letting me know'.

I rang off. I could see at a glance that no one had left any telephone messages. The two men had not rung, so they were on their way. Not police, that was clear. Police would have no need to ask about dialling codes. Mr Bruce had called me at once, which meant that the men could not make it here until at least another hour and a half. The alarms I had at every door and window were already set, and my safe was secured. I lingered over taking some traditional refreshment before locking up and going out to drive the E-Type into a safe corner in the village where it could not be seen by anyone who did not know exactly where to look. I took out from the garage instead my late mother's elderly Vauxhall. Nondescript as it was, this was the ideal vehicle for sinking into the landscape. Dishonest in appearance, admittedly. Since my mother's day, the Vauxhall motor had acquired a sudden surge in horsepower and flexibility. More usefully still, I had optimized weight distribution and replaced suspension units all round with components allowing the harmless-looking saloon to be whipped through bends like a Formula Three car leading its event at Knockhill. I might not need these qualities today, but any time that I did, I knew that I could rely on the Vauxhall to give any opposition a nasty shock.

Anyone coming from the Bruces would arrive along the road that also led from Glasgow. I drove the Vauxhall for half a mile in the Glasgow direction, reversed uphill along a farm road to a point where I could watch my own house through the binoculars kept underneath a seat, and settled down. I did not want anyone bent on villainy to be deterred by thinking that I was at home and prepared for callers. My visitors should find an unoccupied house with an empty garage and believe me to be miles away.

From where I sat, I had an uninterrupted view of the front of my house and the path leading up to it. Trees that had been planted by my late father prevented my seeing the back of the house or the front of the double garage, but I was satisfied to be able to check exactly who came and went.

My callers were in no hurry. It was an hour and forty minutes before they passed the end of the track where I was waiting. They tucked their car close into a bank topped with a hedge, some thirty yards past the entrance to my drive. I watched as two men alighted. Even at that distance my Zeiss binoculars – once German U-boat issue – showed me the first man clearly. I had seen him before. A nose like a quadrant. In my mind I at once named this man MacNeb. Yet it was the other man's face that made me draw in my breath. Dr Bruce's lookalike. What in my young days we should have called a double. The same light brown wavy hair, as far as I could see the same type of round face, and – this was the clincher – the same steel rimmed spectacles.

Together, MacNeb and the Lookalike walked up to my front door, rang the bell and waited. After barely a half minute, MacNeb went alone towards the back of the house, where I could not see him. He returned in a little under ten minutes. The conversation that followed between the two appeared to be intense, then was broken off as if by abrupt agreement. They turned to return to their car.

I started my motor, pulled on an old bunnet that hid both hair colour and head shape, and began to roll back down to the road. At the end of the farm track I turned towards Glasgow. I had travelled a dozen miles before my visitors' car came into view in my rear mirrors. Allowing my speed to vary naturally round Argyll's crests and curves, I was able to keep the other vehicle in sight by maintaining a more or less constant distance between the two of us. This was what I called following from the front. No point letting them see me moving off behind their car and sticking to them like a leech. By letting them come from behind me, I avoided any suspicion. This was a technique that could of course not be used in urban areas, but only on roads such as the present one, leading for miles in the same direction.

I kept ahead of the men's car until the fast dual carriageway leading into Glasgow. Here I let them pass me. They zoomed ahead. As we neared the heart of the city, I closed up the distance between us.

As the traffic lights turned red at Anniesland Cross, they shot through in a tyre-screeching turn towards the Clyde Tunnel. I had more than sufficient power under the bonnet, but a van had pulled in front of me, and my pursuit was over.

I doubted that the number of the men's car would lead me very far. I was right. My police friend Nick reacted with evident alarm when I telephoned him. Was I still poking around in that railway death? I could practically feel his relief when I explained that I wanted help only with a car registration number.

My mobile phone rang a quarter of an hour later. Nick. The car that had lost me at Anniesland was one stolen from Easterhouse. It had just been reported abandoned, off London Road.

Where off London Road?

I was there in ten minutes.

A police patrol was parked at the end of the street where the car stood. Two constables sat waiting, presumably for the arrival of the vehicle that would tow in the car for forensic examination. While they exchanged words in desultory fashion, I managed a little forensic examination of my own. In through the door on the policemen's blind side, I had steering wheel, gear knob and inside door handles dusted in little more than a minute. Nothing, not a scrap of anything, had been left in glove compartment or door pockets. Flooring under the seats was bare.

That would be a nice surprise for the forensic boys, finding the fingerprint areas already dusted. I hoped that little trouble would result for the coppers in the patrol car.

160

IX

ONLY a year earlier, I had discovered a restaurant in Glasgow where venison was better cooked than anywhere else outside Dunoon. I am not going to be idiot enough to betray its location, but shall content myself with recording that I drove to the restaurant before setting off for home.

Finding that I should have to wait for the red deer haunch, I reckoned nonetheless that it would be well worth the delay.

More things would depend on the wait than my gastronomic satisfaction, but I could not know this.

I was right about the cooking. It was every bit as good as I remembered. I lingered over the meal, recalling the occasion when I had introduced Anna to venison. It had never proved to her taste, and our shared favourite remained Chateaubriand.

I had probably not spent so long over a meal since Anna's death. Dawdling as I did meant that I was late in heading out of the city.

Most of the day had been fine, but this was Britain. Decent weather could not be expected to last.

It didn't. I left Glasgow into a hefty downpour, needing from the off to set my windscreen wipers to their highest speed.

Despite the poor visibility, the dual carriageway had me through Dumbarton, past Alexandria and at the foot of Loch Lomond in no time. Tarbet, a village well along the loch's shore, was where I needed to turn away from the water and head off westwards through Arrochar before reaching the southbound road that would – eventually – lead me home.

While still a half mile from Tarbet I could see that there was something wrong. Orange lamps at the junction. No flashing blue lights, so not an accident. A red sign just visible through the rain. 'Road closed beyond Arrochar'.

I stopped. A man in yellow oilskin coat and hat appeared at the car door. I wound down the window a fraction.

'Are you heading into Arrochar?'

'No'. I told him where I had to go.

The man shook his head, sending raindrops through the window onto my face. 'Not your lucky day. Landslip again at the Rest'.

I cursed. The junction past Arrochar where I had to turn was at the crest of a hill known picturesquely from the days of travel on foot as the Rest and Be Thankful. Landslips from the hill above the spot were frequent, with the local council seemingly powerless to prevent repetition.

'How long will it take this time?'

'Couple of days, at least'.

'Thanks'. Damned nuisance, but nothing for it. I closed the window and slid the motor back into gear.

It was just about completely dark by this time, and there were ten more miles to be covered alongside the loch. On other roads, anyone can put ten miles behind him quickly. I don't recommend haste on Loch

Lomondside. North of Tarbet, the road is a switchback. Up and down, left and right, low gear all the way, eyes sharp for the edges of the road and those many spots where it is all too easy to slide right off the tarmac and down into the water.

The loch behind me at last, I had the length of Glen Falloch to drive before reaching the critical West Highland junction of Crianlarich. From here I headed north-west as far as Tyndrum, where the road carries on through Glencoe to Fort William. This was not where I was going. I turned due west as though on my way to Oban.

Curse that landslip! By now I should have been at home, and having a look at what mischief MacNeb had played there. No point moaning, though. We were all at the mercy of the forces of nature, and that was that.

The road I needed branched off a couple of miles beyond Dalmally. This was another slow one, first curving this way and that along the line of Loch Awe, then meandering from one end of Glen Aray to the other. In daylight, the bends in the roads I was traversing were a sheer delight. In the dark – and the wet – they represented the acme of treachery.

The rain, I thought, was heavier than ever. Impatience was not going to help. Sensible hurry in these conditions demanded not just concentration but restraint, as well.

The streets of Inveraray, when I arrived, were empty. This was no night for hanging around, and nobody was doing so.

I knew every yard of the roads around this particular arm of the North Atlantic. One of them would take me home. By the time I reached it, I had completed a modest circular tour of West Highland landscapes that by day were enchanting but in darkness and rain became invisible. But for that landslip, I should have been at the same spot after a mere short, comfortable amble from Tarbet and the shore of Loch Lomond.

Starting with my final trip to police headquarters, it had been quite a day. I was tired, and found myself covering the last miles home on automatic pilot.

The rain was heavier than ever.

Now lightning.

And the flash was persisting. Some poor devil's barn set on fire by it? No. The sound was wrong. That was never thunder. Thunder is a crash. This was a boom.

It took another couple of seconds, then the penny dropped. There was no mistaking the direction. That was an explosion at my house.

I pushed the accelerator without mercy, swung from side to side of the road, tried to make straight lines of the bends.

At my gateway I made a mess of braking, slithered on to the verge at the lochside, away from the house. What mattered: the house was not on fire. The garage was ablaze, or rather, what was left of it. A full blown explosion had destroyed the building. The remains were still burning. Bright flames defied the rain, pungent smoke marked where I had stacked ten winter tyres.

The house remained untouched. Above the doors of the double garage was where MacNeb had planted his bomb. Had I opened either of those doors, I should not now be writing these words.

And I had cursed the landslide that delayed my arrival.

Before police arrived, I needed to see what else MacNeb had done. Scratches on the lock of my back door showed me that he was no expert as a housebreaker.

The bug he had placed in the telephone was of the simplest kind, purchasable at practically any electronics store. I removed the thing, wondering whether I had been meant to find it, whether coming on it was intended to reassure me, while the real bug was concealed somewhere in a more sophisticated location.

I spent the next three quarters of an hour doing an electronic sweep of all the rooms where my speech could be heard. There was nothing. Doubtless I had been crediting MacNeb with too much technical knowhow.

Later I was to realize how wrong I had been in this assumption.

Television camera crews arrived ahead of the explosives experts despatched by police at Dunoon.

My beloved E-Type was well concealed in the village, and I took care to keep its existence from the television news people. As far as they were concerned, my transport was the sedate Vauxhall that had once been my mother's daily runabout.

It did not take the boffins long to determine exactly what explosive materials had been used to generate such destruction. What kept them working, they told me, was the need to discover what had triggered the detonation. That would interest me, too.

Late on the following day, a police superintendent stepped before the television cameras to announce that an animal or bird might have set off the explosion at Mr Greig's home. A bomb appeared to have been attached to the roof of the garage, near the front, with a tripwire running down to both doors. A squirrel, perhaps, or even a large bird, might have activated this tripwire. Officers could confirm that no human remains were found among the wreckage.

That would disappoint two gentlemen I could describe.

The telephone rang just when I was beginning to think about bed.

'Ian'. The voice belonged to Nick. The tone did not. Not to the Nick I thought I knew. Heartiness had been replaced by uncertainty, self-assurance by apology.

'I'm sorry, Ian. We can't make it this weekend'.

'I'm sorry, too. What about next weekend?'

This time the meaning in the hesitation was unmistakable. 'I, I don't think we're going to be able to travel at all, Ian. Joan is not very well, and...'

I rang off with: 'I hope she'll soon be better' and went to bed.

No further word was needed. After all, we had fought major wars to make the world safe for hypocrisy.

X

THE doorbell woke me from deep sleep. Whoever rang was determined that I should not fail to hear it. On and on the ringing went, until I switched on the light over my bedside cupboard. Then the bell ceased. How many, I wondered, were keeping my windows under observation? Easy enough to find out.

Sorry, but my house has none of the installations that one might see in a fictional spy film. No laser detection systems, no cylinders of sinister gas to disable an intruder, not even any impenetrable steel doors. None of those devices without which the fictional agent, even a retired one, seems unable to function.

As I pointed out in a previous memoir, none of us is a superman. Nor are we fitted out by a beneficent Service with every improbable gadget imaginable to the adolescent mind.

I was not going to turn my home into a fortress. All the same, while my mother was alive I had taken one or two elementary precautions as much for her protection as for any other reason. Such measures, though, were little more than anti-burglary safeguards. Our family home did, after all, stand in a somewhat isolated location.

Modest as it was, the little equipment that I had fitted came in useful now. Without revealing myself I could see that the house was surrounded.

A handful of policemen guarding my back door. In the road at the front three police vehicles, one a large estate car, unmarked but unmistakeable.

Nick had known about this, and of course, been unable to warn me. Poor chap. That was why he had been compelled to cancel our socializing. And I had been thinking dreadful thoughts.

I almost laughed, Instead, I retained what I hoped was an expressionless demeanour, flung on a dressing gown and went to the front door.

'Ian Baxter Greig?'

The man putting the question wore plain clothes. He was not a local officer, not one I recognized. Behind him stood three further plain clothes men, flanked by a half dozen officers in uniform. Two of these were women. What on earth? Who did they think was here in the house with me?

Apart from the women officers, we had been here before. The last time a plain clothes policeman asked me at my door to answer to my name, we had flown off together to Craigard. The collection of officers here now meant something very different.

'I have a warrant to search these premises, and must ask you to accompany me for questioning concerning the abduction of Janine Alexander'.

'Well, we all make mistakes'. And if they thought they could throw me off balance, that was another one.

Dr Bruce's fiancée abducted. I knew now why the women officers were here. Did they think that I had her imprisoned in my own home?

The whole ridiculous exercise did at least mean one thing. It left me with not the smallest doubt now that the murdered doctor had been on completely the right track. The dying Simon Grant had indeed been mixed up in something nasty, though how on earth his accomplices thought that abducting Janine could help them once her fiancé was dead, I could not imagine.

As it happened, I knew something about abductions. Had to do with more than a few of them in Berlin. They had been a bit of a speciality of the other side, though I have to admit to having turned the tables just once or twice. Most amusingly of all, I had dragged one of Russia's leading thugs from outside a country hotel in Austria and seen to it that he landed in Britain. Not on my own, of course. I had two of our Service heavy-weights to apply the muscle.

'Please, gentlemen', I invited, 'come in. Just give me a minute or two to toss on some clothes, and I'll be with you'.

They didn't wait for that. I was with them from then on. Two officers stayed in the room with me while I dressed. Even before I was finished, another arrived to begin executing the search warrant among my clothes and shoes. Everything that I did not put on went into plastic bags for laboratory examination. Everything, that is, except for my kilts and whatever else belonged to Highland dress. Almost a tip there, I thought. If you're going to do anything wicked, do it in a kilt. The police will never think of checking your Highland gear. They assume it to be ceremonial wear only.

I could see why they had brought what was practically a demi-van with them. They were going to take away everything they could damned well carry from house and grounds. Jolly good luck to them.

Seek and ye shall find. Or perhaps not. They could turn this house and garden inside out and were not going to come across anything in the least incriminating. Janine's address and telephone number, along with a couple of hundred others, in my contacts book. A file on Dr Bruce's death. Newspaper cuttings, printed-out notes on my conversations with his parents and with Janine. All in a folder in a drawer at the bottom of a desk. Let them make something out of that lot.

I remembered that Nick had once mentioned how police preferred to have the householder present when they were executing a search warrant. This was not a rule of police procedure, he said, but had established itself as a favoured practice. Not always possible, of course, if a suspect living alone was already in custody.

It took them most of the morning. Kept a close eye on me, of course, tapped parts of the walls and floors. Wasting their time.

'If you'll just come with us, sir'.

The ride was comfortable, the reception less so. They did not take me to divisional headquarters in Dumbarton. The police office in Dunoon was where they frittered away precious hours interrogating me.

If Janine had been abducted, they needed all their manpower for tracking her down. Why waste effort on me? They could not seriously believe that I was involved. If I were, did they expect me to have kept incriminating materials in my home?

I was inured to futile questions. Top men in my own Service had held me for grilling on an absurd suspicion of treason. German police had detained me for several days believing that I had murdered an old colleague and friend. Nothing that could be thrown at me now was going to matter a damn. I knew how to withstand the storm.

'When did you last see Janine Alexander?'

'Was she alive when you left her, or was she already dead?'

'Did you kill her accidentally?'

'Was it one of your accomplices who killed her?'

'Where were you between the morning of the 13th and the evening of the 22nd?'

'We'll need every detail, every minute of every day. Write it all down. We've plenty of paper. Just make sure you cover everything'.

'Who were your accomplices?'

'Let's have their names, telephone numbers, addresses, everything you know about them. You help us, and we'll help you'.

'Tell us where you put her body'.

'If you didn't mean to do it, you've nothing to worry about. Manslaughter is treated very leniently these days – particularly if you cooperate'.

'Where is Janine Alexander?'

'Tell us where she is, and we'll see to it that the procurator goes easy on you'.

'Where did you pick her up?'

'Surely you didn't do it on your own?'

'Who helped you?'

171

'How many of you were there?'

'Where did you take her to?'

'Is she in the same place now, or have you moved her about?'

Jumping from one topic to another, and repeating them all endlessly. At least they played me the compliment of not trying on the bad cop, good cop routine. Just stuck with bad cop, bad cop. I played them a compliment, too. I did not demand a lawyer. They were not going to get anything out of me. I knew nothing about the poor girl's abduction. And because I knew nothing, I could not possibly trip myself up. Lawyer unnecessary.

'What can you tell us about this?'

I couldn't tell them a thing. 'This' was one of those key ring attachments sold by motor accessory shops and given to the unfortunate as birthday or Christmas gifts. With a raised Jaguar Cars badge. It was new to me.

'Your name is on it and you haven't seen it before?'

My name on the back, eh?

'Many other Ian Greigs, are there, who own Jaguars?'

'Haven't a clue'.

'We have. The Driver and Vehicle Licensing Authority in Swansea confirms that you are the only one. You are the only Ian Greig who owns a Jaguar, your name is on this tag, and it is not yours?'

'It is not mine, and I have never seen it before. You're not going to tell me that it has my fingerprints on it, are you?'

No. They stopped short of that.

'May I see it?'

As though it were one of Her Majesty's tiaras, interrogator number one dropped the thing into a clear plastic bag, sealed this and handed it across the table.

'Don't want you claiming that we obtained your fingerprints by a trick, do we, sir?'

The job had been very skilfully carried out. Even through the plastic I could see that care had been taken to give the tag a worn appearance as though it were several years old. A short leather strap that was attached, evidently for fastening to the key ring itself, was torn at the far end. The impression was that after years of use the leather had given way at its connection, causing me to drop the trinket.

Very neat. Except for one thing. The forger, or forgers, had engraved the plain back of the badge with the name Ian Baxter-Greig. I had dropped the hyphen years before buying the E-Type. When I was 17, as it happened, and I had never before that owned any Jaguar. Despite the error in the name – they must have gone back practically to birth certificates for that one – the job had been well done. The engraving was not one of those surface scratchings, but a properly deep cutting. Even through the plastic, I could see how much trouble had been taken to age the sunken lettering. Nothing remained of the inevitable shine of newness.

'Might I enquire where you found this?'

'Been wondering where you lost it, have you? Well, we're always pleased to help. It was trodden into the flower bed alongside the path to Janine Alexander's front door. Dropped it just before you grabbed her, no doubt'.

I laughed. I was amazed that a sheriff could have granted a search warrant on such flimsy circumstantial grounds. A weapon of misconstruction.

'Is that your evidence?'

'Oh no. We have an eye witness'.

Of course. They would have, wouldn't they? Anyone taking the trouble to fake up a car key fob would not neglect to provide an eye witness.

'You were seen bundling a woman into your car outside Janine Alexander's home'.

'And this was?'

'Just after ten p.m. on the night of the 13th'.

While I was at home with not a soul to confirm the fact.

'I look forward to seeing this witness in court'.

My chief persecutor, whose name was Campbell, looked embarrassed. I had called his bluff neatly. Oh, he would have an 'eye witness', all right. Needed one to lay before the sheriff for his search warrant. But I bet he never told the sheriff that his 'witness' was an anonymous telephone caller who described seeing a woman being bundled into an E-Type, then rang off without giving his name.

All illogical, anyway. If I had wanted to abduct Janine, I had only to call her. Just claim that I had found out something vital about her fiancé's death, and she would have come running. No need to 'bundle' her into my car.

I had an idea that they could not hold me for more than forty-eight hours without preferring a charge, and knew that no charge could follow without solid evidence. I was right about the charge, but mistaken *re* the time limit. They can go to seventy-two hours before having either to charge or to release a suspect. Still, at least they were feeding me better than my own Service had done when I was briefly under suspicion at Haedquarters. I preferred, though, the coffee given me by the German police to the tea that was habitually served up at Dunoon.

Halfway through that third ridiculous day, a detective crept up to my interrogators to whisper in an ear.

'Interview suspended at 13.37'. Scooping up his papers, Campbell swept them and his junior from the room.

A uniformed constable returned me to my cell. By this time I felt myself quite an old hand at awaiting the pleasure of accusers. I knew well how to occupy my mind for hours at a stretch.

It was something more than three hours later when the same constable who had brought me looked in at the door. 'You are free to go'.

I did not expect an explanation, and that was just as well.

No one from CID thought fit to appear while a desk sergeant handed me back my minor personal belongings – wallet, watch and so on. I signed a receipt and expected to be taken home.

I had spent my nights in the cell wondering about Janine and how she had been abducted. Was she even still alive?

What did my sudden release mean? Had the real villain been apprehended? Had Janine escaped or been released? Either way, she would have confirmed that I had not been involved.

Doubtless a lawyer would tell me that I was entitled to an explanation, if not also to an apology. What I received instead all but rendered me speechless.

'I'm sorry, sir, but the Chief Constable must see you'.

'No need to be sorry'.

'It means a trip to headquarters, I'm afraid'.

It turned out that I was not to see the Chief Constable, after all. Nor even a Deputy Chief. It was one of the Assistant Chiefs.

This was a man determined to impress that his was the commanding position. With every word his manner added 'and don't you forget it'. I knew the type well enough.

'I have received serious complaints about you, Greig. One of my divisional commanders' – oh, they were his, were they? – 'has reported to me that you have been interfering in police business. You have been demanding to see evidence in cases that have absolutely nothing to do with you. You have no official status and categorically no right to interfere in any police matter whatsoever. I understand that in your late employment you were always unreliable. You ran down the department that you headed to such an extent that once you had gone they had to wind it up. May I remind you that departmental heads in your old Service are usually recognized with a medal when they retire. You were given nothing. That, as even you must realize, speaks for itself. You were a failure and an embarrassment to the Service which had the misfortune to employ you. You are not going to embarrass anyone here. In future you will keep away from this building and from everyone employed in it. Any breach of this instruction will result at the very least in a charge of wasting police time'.

And so on.

Of course it was true that I had no right to access police files. I was an outsider with no standing higher than that of any other ordinary subject of Her Majesty.

Yet who was behind this excoriating tirade? It was true that my former offices at Twelvetrees had since been closed. Staff and the work of the department had been transferred to, and incorporated in, that of London headquarters. A fine new building had long since been erected near the Thames, capable of housing every division and branch.

I had given my life to the Service, all my energy, all the creative and analytical thought that I could muster. Like everyone else, I had stuck my neck out for my country. I had not looked, would not look for thanks, but found damnation unwarranted.

Now just who in my old Service would speak to such an extent out of school? If it were to get back at me, I could think of quite a few. Nothing easier than blackening someone's name. Goodness knows, I had done plenty of it myself, spreading misinformation to make the Commies mistrustful of their own people. Could scarcely complain of what was happening to me now. Just curious about it.

Throughout the Assistant Chief Constable's harangue I thought I could read in it the man's own character manifesting itself. All an absurdly elaborate performance to warn me off. Someone somewhere wanted to hide the facts of the investigation into Dr Bruce's death. Yet whoever the meddler, he was too late. I had already seen all the papers and examined such physical evidence as there was – the briefcase sliced in half, along with the doctor's shredded and bloody clothes. And in all of it there was nothing to point me towards a definitive solution.

Now the girl who had been the doctor's fiancée had been abducted. What was the object of that? And why had I been framed, except to put an end to my inquiries?

For the moment, at least, I had no answers.

At home, a message was on my answering machine.

'Hallo, Mr Greig. This is Janine Alexander. I've a lot to tell you. Can you come to our house? Or we could go to a café somewhere and talk. Please give me a call. I do want to see you'.

And I very much wanted to see her. I telephoned at once.

XI

T HE Willow Tea Rooms in Sauchiehall Street were where my father had proposed to my mother, and where my mother in her widowhood had taken tea whenever she undertook a shopping trip to Glasgow. I had been introduced to this architectural gem at an age so early that I have no memory at all of my first visit.

Yet circumstances that in retrospect appear inexplicable prevented my ever taking Anna to enjoy tea amid the unique decor of Charles Rennie Mackintosh. To compensate, perhaps, for this omission, I now treated myself to tea at the Willow whenever my visits to Glasgow permitted me the time.

Reasoning that after her abduction she needed some considerable aid in the cheering up line, I took Janine to the Willow and let her talk. My motive, as you will guess, was not all altruism. Put off guard in the relaxing surroundings of those unique rooms, I knew that she would tell me more than in any question and answer session at home.

Picking up the girl at Helensburgh gave me once again quite a jolt. Janine looked so much like Anna, and today had done her hair in one of Anna's styles. Once she began to speak, any illusion was dispelled. The girl had a controlled, gentle voice, but there was nothing in it of Anna's urbane refinement.

All I knew of Janine's abduction was what the police had told me – that she had been seized on the front doorstep of her parents' home. Bad enough, though not to be compared with what had happened to Anna's mother in Russia – swept from a city sidewalk into a car and raped. That rape, by an infamous figure, had produced Anna.

For Janine, a car had been waiting at the kerb. It was as simple and as blatant as that. Her eyes were bound as soon as the door was closed, and from then on she saw nothing of her abductors. That there were two of them – the driver and the man who pulled her onto the back seat – was about the limit of the information that she could give.

Two men. The same two who had visited the dying Grant in hospital? Who had paid my home a clandestine visit? Did one of the men, I asked, wear glasses?

The driver, Janine thought, might have done. She was unsure.

The one named Bruce?

She couldn't say.

Had any names been used between the two?

No. They had been scrupulously careful about that.

Though I am setting down Janine's account in the form of question and answer, this is not how I obtained the story. What I record is a distillation of what emerged naturally from our *tête-à-tête* without my subjecting the girl to anything resembling an interrogation. I made sure that everything passing between us was on a conversational level. The girl would already have faced enough confrontational questioning from our police friends. Putting her through that again would have served no purpose whatever.

Where did the car take her?

To a house in the country.

How did she know that it was in the country?

Because everywhere was silent. There were no traffic noises, no sounds other than those of the two men.

How was she kept there?

She was confined in one room with window boarded up, but had access to an adjacent lavatory.

Was she able to move anywhere else in the house?

No. A solid wooden door cut off her room and the lavatory from the corridor beyond.

What about a window in the lavatory?

It too was boarded solidly shut. Very heavy boarding. More like planks.

So she had no way of seeing in what part of the country the house was situated?

None at all.

How far did she estimate that the men had driven her after they picked her up?

It seemed to her that they had driven for about an hour before stopping, but she was willing to concede that it could have been twice that. She was in a state of shock, afraid and, of course, blindfolded.

Was the road to the house hilly, full of bends, or did it appear to be reasonably flat and straight?

Flat and straight until they were almost there. Just in the last few minutes they slowed down, took one or two turns and seemed to be climbing a little.

What was her accommodation like?

In itself, comfortable. A decent bed, a table and an easy chair.

And she never saw either of the men's faces?

No. Whenever they came in, they had stockings over their heads.

Either face with a big nose? Well yes, now that you mention it.

Any sign of spectacles? Glasses worn inside a stocking?

Janine laughed. 'Whatever would that have looked like? That would have been a scream'.

She paused. I was sure that I saw a tear. 'You know, that's the first time I've really laughed since, since...'

I touched the girl's hand for a moment. 'I know'. Yes, I did know about bereavement. I waited a few seconds before resuming our talk.

What about the way the men spoke?

One an Edinburgh man, she thought, the second from somewhere in the Central Belt, well west of the capital.

Any mannerisms that were distinctive?

No. They just stood there and put questions one after the other.

What did they want to know?

They were convinced that her fiancé had given her papers belonging to them that they urgently needed.

And had he?

No. But they wouldn't believe her. They went, she said, 'on and on' about papers that she had never seen.

How was she fed?

One of the men, wearing a stocking mask, brought in meals on a tray.

Did she ever see either of the men without a mask, even partially, if a mask slipped?

Never.

Any hint that one might have worn glasses?

None.

How did she break free? Or did the men relent, and open the doors?

They certainly did not relent. They remained convinced that Janine had papers from her fiancé, and that she was simply proving too obstinate to break down.

Her impression was that in another day they would have, as she put it, 'turned nasty'. Resorted to torture was what she meant.

Janine was rescued by a young locksmith named McCulloch. Janine gave me his business phone number, and I determined to call the fellow next morning.

I pulled out my wallet and looked round for Ashley, our waitress, who had been not just friendly and courteous but also outstandingly helpful, as usual.

As I sought for the girl's blonde hair, piled up in a head bun, I caught a pair of man's eyes fixed on me. On the instant, the eyes shifted their focus away.

The evasion was too late. It was impossible for me to forget the face to which those eyes belonged. A face dominated by a nose suggestive of a full quadrant. I flashed a look round. No one with steel rimmed glasses was near MacNeb. No Lookalike. MacNeb was here alone.

Over the years I had looked into the eyes of enough opponents to know when one of them was afraid, when he knew that I had caught him out. MacNeb was not afraid. Even so, now he knew that I had spotted him, he was hurrying outside.

I went after MacNeb as quickly as was consistent with courtesy towards my companion.

The man had been too fast for me. Along the length of the street, to left and right, no sign of him.

Janine appeared not to have noticed the figure with the remarkable nose. She had no idea why I had rushed away. Someone else had taken her attention.

'That waitress', she said, when I returned, 'has the most extraordinary eyes'.

She was right. Ashley's eyes were a mixture of green and brown. What people usually call hazel. But it wasn't their colour that caught the eye. It was their shape. These were oriental eyes in a Scottish face. A more remarkable effect than I am capable of describing.

I attracted the girl's attention and asked whether MacNeb were a regular customer.

'Oh no, sir. I've never seen him in here before'.

This lent some weight to my suspicion that MacNeb had spotted Janine or both of us on our way here, and simply followed. His weakness was that, like all amateurs, he had no idea how to react – or rather how not to react - when I caught his eye.

Next time I saw him I hoped that he would be in the company of a man wearing steel-rimmed glasses. Those two had something to do with the murder of a man I had known and liked, a man to whom I owed a debt for outstanding care.

They were not going to escape.

Two nights after that briefest of encounters I was back again in the Willow Tea Rooms, this time in the company of both Janine and the locksmith McCulloch, who had freed her.

I liked the man at once. He told his story of discovering and liberating Janine in simple and direct terms, entirely without swagger. I appreciated, too, the reserved and courteous way in which he asked whether my full name happened to be Baxter-Greig.

McCulloch owned one of those High Street shops that cuts keys, carries out engraving and repairs the heels of shoes. The same man who had brought him a Jaguar key fob to engrave with my name ('barely medium height, wavy hair, steel-framed glasses') had also engaged him to replace a dodgy lock in the front door of the cottage where Janine had been confined.

It seemed that Dr Bruce's lookalike was the active one. The locksmith never saw MacNeb.

McCulloch carried out the work requested, then a few weeks later was approached again to fit a lock to an internal door 'directly inside the entrance' to the cottage. He promised to attend to this task next day, but was prevented by a telephone call telling him that his brother's death from a brain tumour was imminent. McCulloch drove to his brother near Inverness, not returning to the cottage with his toolbox until three days later. He found no outward sign of occupation, and his knock was not answered.

Nonetheless, anxious not to lose any further time on the promised job, McCulloch let himself in using a master key to the front door lock that he himself had newly fitted.

There could be no mistake about which internal door required his attention. It was, as described, directly facing him. The door was of plain wood, new and unpainted, fitted with bolts top and bottom. Unbolting it, McCulloch was surprised to find how dense and heavy was the wood.

His next surprise was in the whimper that he heard on pulling open the door. Janine was not directly behind it, but crouching frightened in a room off the hallway that this new door abbreviated.

McCulloch would have been inclined to disbelieve her story of abduction, had it not been for the sheer strength of the fresh door that kept her trapped and of the wood that closed off the windows in her room and in the lavatory.

Janine had heard her captors drive off that morning. When she heard McCulloch's car she thought that they had returned, and was fearing further interrogation.

It was fifteen miles to the nearest police house. McCulloch pulled up there with Janine and helped her inside. By this time, Janine was weepy and almost collapsing onto him. The constable having been called away, his wife offered meanwhile to take in the pair and to 'give the girl a nice cup of tea'.

'I just wanted to be telling it all to a policeman, without any waiting', Janine told me. 'So we went to the police station at Callander'.

'Took forty-five minutes', explained McCulloch, 'but at least Callander was in a position to send a carload of men to the cottage'.

Where they arrived too late. Janine's captors had meanwhile returned, found that Janine was free and performed the traditional vanishing act. Traces of gunpowder were found in one of the rooms. They had stored powder there, and had the nerve to wait and take it with them when they fled.

I wasn't going to be able to look at any police reports on this one, but I could find out things for myself.

No question of mistaking McCulloch's description and going to the wrong cottage. Yellow 'crime scene' tape all round – the clearest possible invitation to casual visitors. No sign, though, of any lawmen.

I parked well short of the place. No point in making police a gift of my tyre prints. The cottage was at the far high end of a road, or of what had once counted as a road, before tarmacadam made its appearance. On every side the tops of hills, mostly bare. Not another building in sight.

The walls of the cottage were a display case of samples from the rocks on which it stood. Out of sight of a high road, and of any other dwelling, it had spared its owner the expense of providing the obligatory jacket of white. Even from some little distance, it was apparent that the boarding up work to some of its windows was substantial. No ordinary timber, this, but cut down planks.

The new lock that McCulloch had fitted was effective and an example of the latest sophistication in these matters. Naturally, it remained no match for the accumulated practice of my lifetime.

Inside, fingerprint dusting had been exhaustive. I did some of my own, too – not because I should ever have access to records, but so that I could make comparisons when I ran into more of our two villains' dirty work.

For the police, Janine's abduction must have appeared without apparent motive. It would probably also have looked like an isolated crime.

I knew for a certainty that there was more to come, and I was going to be there when it happened.

XII

IF you ever find a body, for goodness' sake don't report it to the police. If it turns out to be a murder, the discoverer of the body is automatically the number one suspect. That seems to be the rule.

Evidently on the same principle, young McCulloch came in for the third degree after releasing Janine from her captivity. Finding themselves without leads towards whoever had abducted the girl, police turned their aggressive attentions on her poor deliverer.

Bit of luck that he was able to prove having been in Inverness.

The owner of the cottage where Janine was held had inherited it from his parents. He then leased it out for a year while he spent that time in South Africa. From his agent's description, I recognized the lessee as Grant, the man who had died in hospital from car crash injuries. Hadn't signed the lease as Grant, of course, but as William Brown.

The owner never saw either of the two men who had occupied the building.

Janine was vehement in her confirmation that McCulloch was not one of her captors. Though she had not seen either of their faces, she had seen at first glance that McCulloch was both too well built and too young. In addition, his voice was quite wrong.

Though having arrived at the cottage too late to intercept the villains, the police nonetheless mounted a watch on the approach road. A fruitless exercise in surveillance, but they had to do it.

189

There was a sinister thoroughness about the men's preparations that could not fail to arouse in me some grudging admiration. So far as I could tell through the plastic bag in which the police showed it to me, they had done a good job in ageing the newly engraved letters of my name on the Jaguar key fob.

They had handed their suspect to the police all too neatly, I thought.

It was not a perfect job.

Did the villains know – how could they? – that I had been a patient in the same ward as Grant, that I had heard some of what he said to Dr Bruce when he was mistaken about who was with him? None of his ramblings had meant anything to me. Fears about what I might know were all in the madmen's minds.

Whatever threat they thought that I might be to them, they had reacted with astonishing rapidity in recognizing my suitability as what the Americans name a fall guy. Why, I was tailor-made for the part. While trying to find out whether the doctor had left Janine with anything incriminating, make her disappear and frame me for it.

It had proved impossible to obtain from nurses on the ward even a general description of visitors to Grant's bedside. Nurses had more than enough to occupy their minds, without taking notice of patients' callers. Remembering everything that was important about their patients was enough to demand the full-time concentration of an overworked ward staff.

I invited McCulloch for a drink a few days later, when I told him what I did not feel that I could say to Janine. 'I don't believe those men really believed that

Janine had anything from Dr Bruce. All that questioning was not really serious. They abducted her simply to frame me'.

Of course McCulloch was sceptical. Anyone would have been. 'But why should they want to frame you?'

'Simply to get me out of the way. They knew that I was not satisfied about Dr Bruce's death, and wanted to stop me sniffing around'. I left it at that, did not mention the realistic view that I had formed of the abduction.

'So who are those men, anyway?'

'I don't know, yet'.

No, I didn't know who they were, but I had a good idea why they had killed the young hospital registrar. They thought that Grant, finding himself helpless in bed, might have written down their orders, and that Dr Bruce had taken these with him after Grant's death. It was papers they had sought at Dr Bruce's home, papers they had asked his fiancée about. They had taken what papers there were in the doctor's briefcase, plainly in the belief that these were the most important things that he carried. Then found that they had killed him for totally irrelevant and harmless material.

Naturally, I could say none of this to McCulloch.

We parted like old friends.

Janine telephoned. She and her parents felt guilty about the fact that the police had detained me falsely over her abduction. They wanted to make amends in some degree by inviting me out to dinner. If I would just let them know what date would suit me, and name a restaurant of my choice...

I promised, and hung up in some embarrassment. It was not I, but the young doctor who deserved the family's sympathy. Did he have any chance to fight to the end before being brought down?

It was the doctor's briefcase, chained to his wrist, that convinced Grant's henchmen he had taken notes from the dead man. These, supposedly full of evidence against them, they had determined to recover. They must have tried to take the case from the young doctor when he arrived at Craigendoran station. Had he then resisted literally to the death, despite the fact that what he had in the case was nothing of any consequence?

I imagined the poor doctor fighting all the men's efforts until they knocked him out and left him on the rails for the next train to cut the chain holding his case. Had they tried to force the case from his wrist themselves? Searched the doctor's pockets for the key he had refused to give them? Keys were with Janine and his parents, which they could not know. I had to wonder whether the doctor's use of a chained case was a deliberate ploy to suggest that he was carrying important papers. If so, he must have intended to distract attention from something else. But from what?

Two men had visited Grant. Did one of them wear glasses, and was his Christian name Bruce? Had the other a noticeably curved nose?

I had been banned from police headquarters, but not from the hospital that had attended to my broken neck.

I rang Mr Hill-Forrester.

'I'm sorry, sir. He will be in surgery until late. Is it an emergency?'

'Not at all'. Some poor beggar was in a bad way, if an operation had to go on until late. Another reminder of how very lucky I was myself.

'Can you ring tomorrow, before nine o'clock?'

Of course I could. Did. And was at the hospital well before midday.

I wanted to speak to all the nurses who could tell me anything about visitors to Simon Grant, the road accident victim who had died just before I was released.

Good Lord! It was all such a long time ago. Scores of patients, and hundreds of visitors, since then. All the same, two ward nurses remembered having seen the men, but had not spoken to them. A third recalled directing them to the patient's bed. Did either visitor wear glasses? One nurse had, in her words, no idea. The other two thought that he might have done. What about a man with a large curved nose? Lots of visitors had large noses. Had they heard any names mentioned? No, none at all. How about Bruce? Like the doctor? Can't remember.

Mr Hill-Forrester promised that he would cause enquiries to be made among all the nursing staff, but did not expect any positive results.

Neither did I.

XIII

I HAD two aunts who had each passed ninety, and visits from me were long overdue. They lived some way apart, so that I was able to book hotel rooms in different locations and look forward to an enjoyable circular tour.

For once, the weather cooperated. Not only did windscreen wipers remain idle, but sunglasses, rarely used by me in Britain, found themselves in permanent employment. Highland hillsides were enchanting, and roads mercifully clear. I found both aunts very much *compos mentis*, active and alert to the world. This might have surprised me had I not remembered what a livewire each had always been.

For my homeward trip I decided to allow myself a couple of special treats. A restaurant at Balquhidder used to serve the finest herring in oatmeal that it was possible to find east of Loch Fyne. The dish was no longer available there, but I decided to visit the establishment anyway and take whatever was best on the menu these days. A secondary motive for driving via Balquhidder, which was frankly out of my way, was that it gave me an excuse for flashing over the Duke's Road.

I downed an excellent lunch of smoked haddock with small new potatoes, garden peas, sweet corn and baby carrots. Dessert was nothing that could be taken orally. It came on wheels. A gentle amble down the A84 until turning right through a narrow opening a couple of miles before reaching Callander. This led me along past Loch Venachar as far as Brig o' Turk.

Here at Brig o' Turk begins one of the finest roads in Britain for those who enjoy sheer driving. Built to give access to Montrose's lands, the Duke's Road twists this way and that, up hills and down hills, for a most delicious seven miles, until swooping, bends and all, down into the comfortable town of Aberfoyle.

Not for the first time, I had been a little over eager. Keen to get out into some driving that would be sheer enjoyment rather than merely fulfilling the need to reach the next destination, I had rushed from my Balquhidder table without taking the usual coffee.

No more convenient place to correct this omission than at Aberfoyle. The town has one of the most useful car parks to be encountered anywhere in Scotland – central, spacious, accessible without trouble and adjacent to every kind of business that one might want to visit. I rolled in.

Good, straightforward coffee was to be had, rather than the complex Americanized assortment that seems to be taking over these days. I enjoyed a large cup, then wandered into one of the bigger stores to have a look of the current prices of whisky. This was a beautifully sunny summer weekend and, Aberfoyle being within such easy reach of Glasgow, there were huge crowds in the shops, in the car park and in the town generally.

Sadly, the good whisky was at the wrong price, and vice versa. That's what happens when government interferes with the natural processes of a free market. It looked as though no one at Holyrood had even heard of Adam Smith, let alone read him.

I stepped outside, and there he was. No doubt about it. The Lookalike. Here was the man whom Grant, when he was dying, thought that he had seen in young Dr Bruce. The same lightly wavy hair, roughly the same round face and – this was the clincher – the same steel rimmed spectacles. Grant had heard the registrar addressed by a superior as 'Bruce'. That had started the confusion in the man's fading mind.

There was none in mine. This was the man who had accompanied MacNeb on his bomb-laying visit to my home. 'Bruce', I called. The Lookalike turned, stared for a moment and recognized the expression on my face. He vanished into the crowd.

I had seen the same thing once in Berlin. Four seemingly innocent citizens, ambling along on a peaceful afternoon in a quiet street. A policemen appeared, strolling without purpose, and the four shot off like rabbits startled by a fox. I had never seen people break into a run so quickly as on that occasion.

The Lookalike had vanished as quickly, without needing to run. He was short enough simply to have disappeared into the shelter of a slow moving mass.

I hunted through the crowd for a good ten minutes. Cars were leaving all the while, others arriving. I failed to spot the Lookalike. No doubt he was already on his way back to whatever criminal lair he inhabited.

Too late I thought of watching the car park exit. The bird had flown.

Chance, if it was chance, had let me see the faces of both my enemies. That was something, though little enough.

I drove home in an atrocious mood, hammering the Jaguar every foot of the way. No point owning an E-

Type if she weren't allowed to show me occasionally what she could do. Never, though, when Anna was on board had I pushed it, however tempting the road.

Kicking myself for having let the Lookalike slip away, I settled down to ruminate with a decanter at my elbow. Only now did it occur to me that the man had not so much lost me at Aberfoyle as that I had lost him. Such was my annoyance at losing sight of the Lookalike, I had pushed the Jaguar as hard as I could right from the Aberfoyle car park until I was home. He had evidently watched me set off, then gone on his way well satisfied.

I was in Glasgow next day, once again indulging my liking for venison and not returning until late at night. Among the messages waiting at home on my answering machine was one from Dr Bruce's parents. 'Oh Mr. Greig, we should be so grateful if you could call and see us this evening, please. We have found something of Alasdair's and we don't know what it is. Can you please telephone, and let us know what time you can arrive?'

I thought it too late to telephone the Bruces that night. I did so first thing next morning, and found a recorded message saying that they would be away on holiday for two weeks. So that was why they had wanted to see me the night before, while I was wasting time pretending to be a gourmet. These were the summer holiday months, yesterday had been Friday, and most holidaymakers left home on a Saturday.

A fortnight later I dialled the Bruces' number again. 'When would it be convenient for me to call?'

'Any time you like. How about tomorrow morning? About eleven?'

'Fine'.

'And you'll stay for lunch?'

I did, but it wasn't what I wanted to do. I was far too intrigued by what Mr Bruce had found.

'We decided to re-do Alasdair's room', his father explained. 'We were burgled, you know'.

'Burgled? When was that?'

'About a week after you were here the first time'.

'Five days', corrected Mrs Bruce. Women are always so much better at memorizing details.

'Yes. Five days', conceded her husband.

This had been no coincidence. 'I'm sorry to hear that. Did you lose much?'

'Luckily, there wasn't much taken. Just bits and bobs. No real value. I did notice, though, that papers had been gone through in Alasdair's room. They left a bit of a mess. That's why we decided to chuck out his old furniture and redecorate. Fresh wallpaper, new carpet, the lot. I found this thing tucked under an edge of the carpet, beneath a bedside cabinet. I suppose you know what it is'.

A USB drive, sometimes called a memory stick. Smaller than any I had seen before, outside some of the devices we had used in the Service.

I had searched plenty of rooms, encountering all levels of skill and näivety in concealment. I wondered at the caution the doctor had exercised. He had taken no chances, not even in his own home. Whatever was on that memory stick was probably what his killer or killers had wanted. Yet had the killer even known of the memory stick's existence? Papers appeared to have been the object of the break-in and search. It looked as though the young doctor had stored what he knew electronically, leaving his killers to believe that he was carrying papers. There had been nerve there, but also proof that the doctor knew that he was dealing with real villainy.

One oddity only. There no sign of any computer in the house. His parents swore that he did not have one. Like the typescript of *The Lion's Mouth*, whatever was on the memory stick must have been put there either at the hospital or at Janine's.

The Bruces were well composed and with minds quite made up about their son's death. 'Our boy did not kill himself', his mother asserted. 'That was not in his nature. In any case, if you had seen the way that he was looking forward to his wedding...'

'I do not believe suicide, either', I assured her. 'It's not going to be easy to find the explanation. In fact, I never may. But I should like to try'.

'We are not well off', interposed her husband. 'We can't afford a detective'.

'Mr Bruce', I assured him, 'I am not in business as a detective, nor do I intend going into business as a detective. I want to look into the question of your son's death for my own satisfaction, that's all'.

'But you don't believe that it was suicide, do you?' The registrar's mother was eager, desperate to have what she evidently regarded as a stigma removed from her son's name.

'It seems unlikely', I admitted.

Pressing on with as much restrained urgency as road and traffic conditions permitted, I did not waste time on my drive home. *Allegro ma non troppo,* as a musician would say. Fast, but not too much. Speed – you can believe this or not, as you wish – is not my customary mode on Highland roads, but I was eager to see what was on that memory stick.

Once home, I slid it into a USB port on my laptop. There was only one file on it, entitled *Grandson.* Oh no, I thought. Another literary effort, and it sounds like something autobiographical.

I opened the file anyway. The text was encrypted. What on earth?

However simple the encryption, deciphering was going to require some concentration and mental effort. Though scarcely in the mood for another of Dr Bruce's novellas, or whatever the thing was, I poured myself a 16-years-old malt from Islay, left the decanter conveniently close to my right hand, and set to with old-fashioned but still effective pencil and paper.

Text encryption turned out to be of the simplest kind, not significantly above schoolboy level. No one would be recruited by my late Service who could not decrypt such an effort without instruction.

At first, I wondered whether *Grandson* was a collection of notes for the plot of an intended novel that Dr Bruce had since discarded.

But no. Among the file's properties the author was listed as 'Simon Grant'.

Well, naturally. What did I expect when all was encrypted? Surely not even the most fearful of would-be writers, jealous of his treasured embryo, encrypts his creation.

Even so, my immediate reaction was that the contents were too sensational to be real.

I soon realized that they represented reality. They fitted in with my certainty that Dr Bruce had been murdered.

I also realized that I had misunderstood what I believed to have been Simon Grant's announcement that they would 'show' the Poles.

Grandson was no work of Dr Bruce's. It was a lengthy memorandum. No. More than that. It was a detailed set of instructions written evidently by Simon Grant. What MacNeb and the Lookalike had thought was on paper. Those two were not Poles, though they might have been. Growing up with a Scots accent does not mean that parents have not immigrated from another country. All the same, I knew now that Grant's followers were Scots.

Had Grant, knowing that he was going to die, mistaken Dr Bruce for a co-conspirator and given him the memory stick from his pocket? Or had the doctor abstracted the object from among the dead man's possessions?

However he came by it, had the doctor, too, decrypted the file? Did he know, before he was pushed under that train, that he had stumbled onto a political idea so outrageous as to have little equivalent in British history?

XIV

THE bullet missed me, but left a neat pair of holes in the Jaguar. The damage made me livid as hell. I saw at once that the marksman, whoever he was, had chosen a clever position. I was in the middle of a slow turn when he caught me from what was a rarity in the Highlands – a spot where escape was possible along four different roads.

For the umpteenth time I reflected on the differences between real life and the adventures of the fictional agent. What rotten shots James Bond's opponents must have been! They would not only fail to hit him, but would miss his Aston-Martin as well.

This being reality, I was left instead to suffer the mortification of the devoted owner who has cherished his prized motor through many years without collecting a scratch, only to have some swine ruin things.

I wondered how many hours they had wasted, watching for me. Well, I should not waste time worrying about them. On the other hand, I was not going to take the mutilation of my E-Type lying down.

In contrast to my customarily decorous driving style, I slid to a halt and sprang over the side of the car.

I had not indulged in a good old-fashioned foot chase since well before the Wall came down. It was time to catch up on my arrears of exercise.

Berlin, like Munich, is a disappointingly flat place. I could do no hill running while at Berlin Station, but was able to content myself with circuit after circuit of one of the city's many running tracks, up to the point of exhaustion. I would do this in particular on a Sunday morning, to punish myself for Saturday night's indulgences. Hill running, as in young cross-country days, was possible only during visits home, and, frankly, I was then almost always too busy with other pastimes to do any. Here now was my chance to make up for lost opportunities and to see what I could still do.

With a strong lope, I set off up the hill. Having done plenty of uphill work in those cross-country years, I knew just how to pace my efforts for the slopes ahead.

The place where the shot had been fired was apparent from the angle between the two holes in the Jaguar's bodywork. I had covered probably no more than eighty yards towards the spot when I saw a figure rise against the skyline.

Another shot. It passed nowhere near me. I only hoped that it had not struck the car. I kept running. The figure on the skyline disappeared.

At this point I should like to make it clear that I am not a hero. I should not run towards a Russian sniper. I maintained my chase only because it was obvious that the shooter on the hill was no great shakes as a rifleman – and because I was furious at what he had done to my Jaguar.

There is a certain bloodymindedness in me that used frequently to upset, in turn, my mother, my schoolmasters and my Service superiors. I like to think that it had also led me to do things that had hurt our country's enemies. It pushed me now to keep on running, despite the obvious futility of any attempt to catch a man who had disappeared over the other side of a hill. Futile or not, I modified my pursuit to the extent of heading not towards the top of the hill but around a shoulder of it.

It is dispiriting to be forced to the realization that one is not after all as fit and as young as one has been deceiving oneself that one is. The climb, though nowhere near as steep as it might have been, made noticeable demands on lungs and legs before I was halfway to the skyline point for which I was aiming.

In itself, the strain was nothing unfamiliar. It had, though, set in rather earlier than I expected. Still, I had had plenty of practice in pushing that sort of thing to the back of my mind. Concentrating my thoughts and my vision solely on the skyline spot that I intended to reach, I forced my legs into repetition, repetition, repetition.

Those final strides sagged, but I was there. Below me, at a road junction, two figures were struggling downwards towards a parked car. Perhaps a hundred yards separated them. The figure nearer to the car carried a rifle. While I had been fighting upwards, these two had enjoyed the benefit of a downhill run.

Now it was my turn to take advantage of the downward slope. It is only fair, though, to point out that a downhill route does not necessarily guarantee speed. One needs strong legs and fitness to take advantage. My past running had left me very definitely better equipped in this respect than the other two.

I was halfway down towards the road when the first of the men reached their car. It was the one with a rifle. By this time I could see him clearly. MacNeb. He turned, took a couple of seconds to aim, and fired. It was his third shot at me, and this time I heard the bullet whistle by.

MacNeb tossed the rifle into the back of the car and scrambled into the driving seat. My first thought was that if he had gone round to the far side he could have rested his rifle on the roof to take decent aim at me.

Now the Lookalike reached the vehicle. He turned before climbing in and produced a pistol. The sun flashed for an instant on his glasses. The Lookalike loosed a wild shot vaguely in my direction before climbing into the seat beside MacNeb.

The car was away, and I was left still running down a Highland hill.

Clearly, each of those two lunatics was a complete duffer with firearms. Just what would they try next? They had tried a bomb. Only a sheer fluke saved me. They had tried bullets, but were no marksmen. Each was a stupid act, and showed just how desperate they had become to eliminate me.

Of necessity, the villains were making it up as they went along. Naturally, they were going to slip up sometime.

I began the trudge back to my E-type with murderous feelings. If there were any more holes in it...

The E-Type was OK – if you can describe as OK a car with two bullet holes through its bodywork. What I mean by OK is that no further bullets had struck it.

I should be sending the Jaguar to the best body shop I knew of, from where it would come back like new. Useful to have the car out of the way. There was business for me to do in Edinburgh, where I had rented rooms. No one knew of the place, and it was going to stay that way.

Once they had seen me probing into the young hospital registrar's death, MacNeb and the Lookalike had gone to a deal of trouble to track me down and waylay me.

I certainly was not going to return the compliment.

Search for those two lunatics? I shouldn't bother. All I had to do was wait, and they would show themselves.

The advantage that I had was in knowing what the two intended. They were carrying out the orders of a dead man. Grant had been the prime mover, the organizer. What the others had to do was all in his encrypted file.

There, on the tiny memory stick unearthed by Dr Bruce's father, was every detail of what the murdered doctor had called Grant's 'something nasty'. Well, Grant was dead. He died after skidding into a tree on a wet Aberdeenshire road. Sadly, a commonplace enough occurrence.

Working my way through the decryption of Grant's file *Grandson,* I soon uncovered the answer foremost among those I needed. His 'something nasty' foresaw roles for no more than three men, one of them Grant himself. I had pictured a gang, and all I had to face were two.

I knew their plan, and what they looked like, but not who they were. They, on the other hand, knew where to lay their hands on me at any time. Something had put the villains on to me, alerted them to my interest in their activities. Had they seen me visiting Bruce's parents that first time, while they were casing the house for their burglary? Or had I called on Janine while they were watching her in preparation for the abduction? If they had seen me drive from Janine's straight to the Bruces, that would have clinched in their minds that I was a danger to them.

From their point of view it certainly would make no sense to put Dr Bruce out of the way yet leave me alive. All the same, I went about life's tasks as usual, and no further shots were fired at me. Were they beginning to develop cold feet, had they frightened themselves off?

Murder on a Highland road, particularly of someone with my career background, would have excited police attention of an uncomfortably tenacious nature. British police do not close murder cases – not until a lifetime after the killing, when the murderer can no longer be alive.

I could not be worth the trouble. Just a nuisance to them - though I had proved useful in taking suspicion for Janine's half-hearted abduction.

Why half-hearted? I had not mentioned this either to Janine, her parents or to her rescuer McCulloch, but I believed the girl's seizure to have been no more than a rehearsal, a practice for abducting a nationally important figure at a later date.

Now that they had lost the cottage where they had held Janine, the villains needed to find another, or at least some sort of isolated building, for the serious abduction that was part of their plot.

Grant had put together plans for a series of dirty tricks as diabolical as anything I had experienced throughout the entire Cold War.

The sheer criminality involved might have suggested bringing in Scotland's police. This I had to put right out of the question.

I could expect no help from the police, with whom I was distinctly *persona non grata.* Dr Bruce's father would confirm that he had given me the memory stick, or one like it, but who was to say that I had not myself written what was on it?

Suspicion must remain that the bomb at my garage had been my own work. Yes, police had earlier searched my home and found no bomb-making materials, but these could have been hidden elsewhere or acquired later. Once a person has become what they call 'of interest' to the police, there are no limits to possible suspicions.

I was on my own in this one, and should trust nobody. That suited me just fine. I was used to working alone, and indeed preferred it.

All the same, it was only fair to save Nick the wasted effort of a pointless chase after foreign criminals.

'It wasn't Poles that worried Grant', I told him on the telephone. 'It was polls'.

'Polls? What on earth does that mean?'

'Public opinion polls'. I knew that well enough – now – but how I knew was not something that I was going to share.

The courtesy car loaned to me by the coach builders while they repaired my E-type was a sophisticated new Toyota. More computers on board than a luxury liner.

The remains of my garage had not yet been removed, so that there was not even a forecast of when work might begin on building a replacement. Overnight, the Toyota had to stay in my drive, where plenty of shrubs concealed it from passers-by on the road. The Vauxhall I had transferred to Edinburgh, where I should have work for it to do.

There would be plenty of running round in the Toyota before I returned it with joy in exchange for my E-Type. I tanked up the car fully and set off on a domestic errand through the Highlands. An hour or more from home, there was a familiar kind of figure walking along the roadside ahead. No one I knew, but a type known to me from childhood on. The vagrant who had lost his home. A broken marriage, property gone through repossession by a mortgage lender, surrender to the irresistible need to escape a life drowning in routine. Who knew what had driven these individuals into a life of trudgery, an existence invariably shortened by lack of proper nourishment, persistent exposure to the roughest of weathers, absence of medical care and a dozen other privations? These men were not gypsies. They were not tinkers. They had been raised in environments as ordinary as those that had nurtured the rest of us.

It was a matter of course to offer a lift to those I encountered tramping our Highland roads. I slowed the Toyota and could see at once that here was a man uncomfortably close to the end of a life that can have offered little in the way of joy and much in the way of forced endurance. Though I put his age at not significantly greater than my own, the ravages of his existence were pitiful. What chances might this poor fellow have thrown away?

My own life had been more than fortunate. It had been privileged, at least in the start I had been given. That I had not made more of my opportunities and capacities was my own inexcusable fault.

'Would you like a ride?' I asked through an open window.

'Where are you going?'

As soon as I told him, the man had the door open. I was surprised to see that he brought in with him only a very small pack. An expert in self-sufficiency, this one. Not surprising, though. The man's way was uphill, his steps eloquent of approaching exhaustion. Unsurprisingly, there was not an ounce of fat on his frame. Face not totally emaciated, but gaunt enough. Grey hair, that could easily be dangling untamed, trimmed to a manageable and tidy length. Clothes as clean and well maintained as ever imaginable in a life of tramping through all weathers and spending nights in corners shared with fellow mammals. This man had not surrendered to apathy or abandoned his self-respect.

It was my principle not to question any passengers I picked up. If they wanted me to know anything, they would tell me. It was evident that this man, though not highly educated, had a respectable background. He spoke well and, fighting against the weaknesses that years of sustained adversity had imposed, did his best to maintain some sort of bearing. I liked and respected him.

After all, I should be a poor sort of human if consciousness of my own good fortune did not stimulate sympathy for others markedly less blessed. Had my mother not always reminded me when I was a boy and we had encountered unfortunates: 'One day it could be you in that situation'?

Barely three miles after the spot where I picked up my guest, a hill bend combined with a sheer drop from the edge to create the most perilous stretch of road I knew north of the Devil's Beef Tub. I changed down on my approach to the turn.

Or tried to. The gears simply refused to move from fourth to third. Under my right foot the accelerator pedal dropped away. As engine revs rose, the gearbox shifted not down, but up, from fourth to fifth.

I stood on the brake pedal. It did not move.

We were rushing into the bend. I wrenched on the steering wheel. It would no more turn than the brake pedal would allow itself to be depressed. Controls had seized, and the two of us in the vehicle were helpless.

'Bale out!' I yelled, giving my passenger a shove towards his door. I hurled myself through my own exit. Now I knew how hard a road surface felt when struck at something like ninety miles per hour.

Not satisfied with ninety, the Toyota kept on accelerating and shot out into space. There was no sign of my passenger.

XV

I SCRAMBLED up and hobbled rather than ran to the edge of the road. It was the fastest that I could move after all but making a hole in the tarmacadam. Below, a swelling mass of flames was brightening the hillside halfway down towards the silver burn at its foot.

I searched the slope for my passenger. Nowhere on the ground. The poor man had not left the car, not mercifully been catapulted wide. Had he at least been knocked senseless before the fire took him?

I dropped over the edge, slithered, scrambled, fell and toppled as far as the blazing shell. Impossible that I should see inside. I cowered just outside the radius of unbearable heat. No waiting that I have ever endured could be compared with those appalling minutes watching the end of a car that did not belong to me and of a man whose name I did not even know.

For both I was responsible. Had I not filled the tank to capacity, my innocent passenger might have had a chance. It was my turn for an unflattering by-name, and I gave myself one: MacNumpty. Not that all the self-blame and sense of guilt in the world was going to help.

The flames began to weaken and separate. I peered through them into the interior.

There is no point in describing all that I saw and felt. Each of you will have sufficient experience and imagination to appreciate the horror of that day. It will be enough for me to tell how, once I had seen the fire all but burn itself out and confirmed the ghastliness within, I carried on down the hillside to the glen below.

The day was dry, cool and overcast. Underfoot the ground was firm. I stepped out as strongly as my bruises from the road would allow. Just less than an hour later, I struck another road. In either direction this one led away from where I had been heading in the Toyota. It carried a lot more traffic, and offered the benefit of a transport café a mile from where I reached it. I knew that café from younger days, when it had been a regular stop for lorry drivers. Since then it had changed hands and gone considerably upmarket. It was still, though, a stopping place for long-distance buses. At the café I tidied myself up for a bus that landed me in Perth before dark. A train had me in Edinburgh in such good time that before midnight I was able to watch in my rooms a television report of my death in a car crash. There were pictures of the burned-out car and a statement that my body had been burned beyond recognition.

That was how it was going to stay. I had villainy to prevent, and the villains were not to hear the least suggestion that I was still around to do it. Let them carry on full of confidence that they would pull everything off.

MacNumpty. That was what I had called myself for killing the pitiable fellow man to whom I had given a lift. I should deserve a far worse name if in due course I did not come back to life and own up about the body in the Toyota. Somewhere the man must have family of some kind. They deserved to know what had happened to him.

That was a duty for the future. Meanwhile my mind went to the file named *Grandson.* This laid down, in full operational detail, a plot by a handful of fanatical Scottish Nationalists whose object was to ensure the breakup of the United Kingdom.

It was polls that had upset Grant, not Poles. He had dreamed up his scheme because every public opinion poll and every survey conducted over the past year and a half had shown that scarcely more than a third of Scots voters were prepared to vote for 'Yes' in the forthcoming independence referendum. To overturn their reluctance, Grant had calculated that drastic and dramatic actions were needed.

What he had dreamed up were not propaganda activities, but crimes. To carry them out two other men were required.

The two other men who had visited Grant at his bedside. The two men I had seen together at Aberfoyle. Both had visited my house, one of them planting a bomb. Both had, uselessly, fired shots at me. One, at least, had taken electronic control of the car I was driving, turning it into a write-off and killing an unfortunate man who had accepted a lift from me.

All this had been in aid of the referendum 'Yes' campaign, though exactly how MacNeb and the Lookalike knew that I was a threat to their schemes remained obscure. It was a supposition on their part. If they had anything concrete to justify their fears, I should be very much surprised.

Yet in their asumption, with or without evidence to support it, they were not wrong. I was going to stop them, and now that they believed me dead I was going to find it that much easier.

I had not worked long on *Grandson* before understanding two of the remarks I had caught from the lips of Grant as he lay dying in that hospital bed. 'Doesn't matter' and 'It will be too late' made total sense to me now.

The conspirators' plan, as I read the details on my computer screen, reminded me of what Dr Bruce had written in *The Lion's Mouth* about minds in the grip of an ideology. 'Voluntary mindlessness' was a phrase that he had used, and I reflected how much this applied not only to the blind following of others' ideas. It was equally mindless to allow one's own feelings and convictions to degenerate into extremism.

In the notes he had compiled on the memory stick, Grant had revealed himself, like so many dedicated nationalists the world over, as a man without scruples, a man potentially a killer. A man willing, at least, to encourage others into murder.

I might have almost no information about Grant's henchmen, but I certainly knew where to look for them if I wanted to. On the fringes of the independence movement. On the fringes because I could not believe that the Nationalist party itself would tolerate extremists of the sort that we were dealing with here.

Nonetheless, the likeliest place for clues to the pair must be among party adherents. Fanatics who favoured 'direct action' rather than reliance on the ballot box would make plenty of noise within the independence movement. My best allies would be among those fellow Nationalists whom they had failed to convince. If I wanted allies. Far better on my own, I thought. Though I should probably need some muscle.

SNP fanatics would doubtless be disbelieving, were they to hear that we in Scotland are all nationalists. We adore our country, are infinitely proud of her achievements and hold her second to none on the planet.

We are equally proud of the United Kingdom and her successes, not least of her performance when she found herself alone in 1940 and resolutely carried on. What the UK did in the years following her finding herself alone was triumphant vindication of that prophecy by the last Stuart monarch, Queen Anne. 'By the union', wrote the Queen, arguing for unity in 1706, Britain 'will be enabled to resist all its enemies... and maintain the liberties of Europe'.

Britain certainly did that, and Scots can be as proud of the accomplishments of our United Kingdom as they are of what Scots alone have done. In no way does pride in Britain diminish our sense of identity, which naturally we celebrate and cherish, whether it is as Scots, English, or Welsh.

Yet Nationalist propaganda holds that Unionists basically feel contempt for anyone other than the English and are interested in maintaining the union mainly for England to secure income from North Sea oil and gas. From whisky, too.

If this nonsensical defamation were true, how could any Scot be a Unionist? Yet propagandists will shrink from nothing to win support for their aims. Didn't someone once point out that a big lie is always more readily believed than a small one?

The actions planned by the dead Simon Grant were intended to destroy the campaign for a 'No' vote in the independence referendum through fabrications aimed at discrediting Unionists. So far as I could make out, Grant had not intended to play any part in the physical actions that were planned. His death was in that sense no loss to the plot. Grant's part was to have been in revealing false information to the news media. The two survivors could carry this out just as well.

I had told Mr Hill-Forrester nothing of what was on the memory stick handed to me by Dr Bruce's parents. Strictly speaking, it was of concern to him that one of his subordinate doctors should have taken home some property of a patient. Nonetheless, I thought it enough that he had seen the manuscript of *The Lion's Mouth*, and did not want to raise any further concerns in the mind of an overworked man.

Ignoring even Dr Bruce's murder and the pot shots at me, I might once have been sceptical about the seriousness of Grant's written intentions. It was the mistreatment of the UKIP leader when he visited Edinburgh last year that showed me for the first time the viciousness of Nationalist behaviour. After that display, nothing more could surprise me.

To his Nationalist co-conspirators Grant bequeathed detailed plans for those actions intended to swing the independence referendum solidly in favour of a 'Yes' vote. A Castle was to be attacked with explosives, and the Wallace Monument near Stirling blown up. Both atrocities were to be laid at the door of Unionists. I now understood the words of the dying Grant, who had said: 'Leave the monument alone. Just concentrate on the castle'.

There was also a plan to include the kidnapping of the SNP leader, Scotland's First Minister. This too was to be laid at the door of Unionists campaigning for a 'No' vote. After that business with the UKIP leader, I now knew that such a scheme was all too credible. Janine's abduction had been a practice run for this operation.

Most dramatic of all was a well-prepared design to blacken the name of a leading Conservative Member of the Westminster Parliament, a prime mover in the Unionist 'No' campaign. This man's father had been adopted in the 1920s, the identity of his natural parents remaining a mystery. During the 1950s and '60s, the adopted boy had grown into a leading member of Scotland's business community. It was his son, now prominent in the Westminster Parliament and foremost in founding the 'No' campaign, who was the extremists' principal target.

Grant's men were preparing to announce to the news media that they had solved the mystery of this man's grandparentage. Their solution was, I could see after a little research, perfectly assembled. 'Fits beautifully', Grant had said. I knew now what he meant. Fitted beautifully was just what the details did, as I could read in the *Grandson* file. There were other things Grant had said, too, that must have referred to this scheme. 'All worked out', and 'Dynamite'. It certainly would be that.

According to Grant's notes, Nationalists in key positions in the Scottish press and in broadcasting were expected to slant news stories into separatist propaganda. They were to be issued with guidelines as laid down in *Mein Kampf,* as follows:

'The amount of information the masses can take in is very limited, and their understanding is poor. On the other hand, their forgetfulness is prodigious. For these reasons, all effective propaganda must be limited to only a very few points, and these must be hammered in over and over again like mantras, long enough until every last man understands what he is meant to understand. Whenever this principle is ignored, and any diversity of ideas presented, the result will be that people grasp neither one thing nor the other, since the masses are incapable either of digesting or of retaining what they are told'.

With such a level of contempt for both the public and the individual, who could be surprised that, presumably fearing that he was about to expose their schemes, the conspirators had silenced Dr Bruce?

And who would wonder when the plotters unveiled a top man in the 'No' campaign as Adolf Hitler's grandson?

XVI

IT was an imaginative scheme, there was no denying it, and the plotters had collated their data very thoroughly. Somehow, Grant – or someone else – had come across the case of a young Bavarian woman who had moved to Britain in the 1920s, given birth to a son and put out her baby for adoption. Grant had left to his Nationalist accomplices documents showing that the woman had named the boy's father as Adolf Hitler.

The birth was dated years before Hitler became German Chancellor, and before he had taken up with his niece Angela. At that time, he had not even met Eva Braun, the eventual Frau Hitler, who was then still a young schoolgirl.

As Grant had clearly recognized, 'No' campaigners would be unable to counter the sensation of a Hitler link until the referendum was over, its outcome irrevocable.

Naturally, I was conscious that no one should be held in any way associated with the actions of forebears, particularly not of those whom the individual has never known. At the same time, I was all too clearly aware that some concomitant guilt is exactly what the public does tend to ascribe.

Adolf Hitler's grandson? I could not imagine any reasoned argument in favour of the independence movement that could be more effective with voters than this simple slur.

Why, the man is carrying the seed of Satan. And a creature like that is telling us not to vote for independence? He can go to the devil, where he belongs. And we most certainly *shall* vote for independence.

I had thought much about how easily the poll could be influenced, and realized that no one had mentioned what sort of majority would be needed for independence to be implemented. Two-thirds, perhaps? Sixty per cent? Seventy-five per cent? Why had I never heard any figure reported?

I despatched an e-mail to the 'No' campaign, querying the matter. The answer that I received did not bear the name of any individual, and read as follows:

'Thank you for your e-mail. I believe it is fifty per cent plus one'.

If anyone had told me beforehand that any state, let alone an atomic power and permanent member of the United Nations Security Council, could contemplate breaking up on the simple majority of a single vote from the electorate, I should have told the fellow that he was an idiot. Now, though, I realized that the idiot was whoever had agreed to the referendum without first defining the majority necessary.

'Fifty per cent plus one' represented lunacy to the point of criminality. I understood now how utterly serious was the threat not just to our country but to common sense. How easy, with or without their trio of dirty tricks, was it likely to be for the Nationalists to swing a single vote majority in their favour? Easy not least because they were swelling the electorate with the addition of 16- and 17-year-olds, voting for the first time. Might not these youngsters be too easily influenced by Nationalist romanticism?

After all, even a grown man of the stature of Robert Burns could be deceived by rumour and innuendo. 'A parcel o' rogues' is what he named Scotland's Unionists, who he thought had been 'bought and sold for English gold'.

Poor Burns. They wouldn't have given him access to records in those days, would they? Burns could not know that cash did not find its way across the border. We are luckier today, with public papers available in open archives. If Burns had been given opportunity to study the Treaty of Union, he would have found that while Westminster penned only four of its Articles, Holyrood dictated twenty-five – all to Scotland's advantage. Each of those twenty-five Articles was accepted by Westminster in its entirety. None of this is what would have happened if Scots were being 'bought'. Scotland did well out of the treaty, but that naturally did not stop the gossipmongers, who as usual were able to play on public ignorance. Still, Burns left us with some memorable verses, and we can enjoy these irrespective of the truth.

It was today that Scotland's electorate was up against a parcel of rogues, right enough, though I did not believe for a moment that the SNP leader, or anyone near the top of the party, knew anything at all about the extremists' plot. Nor could I believe that the party leadership would condone the men's actions had these become known.

If I were to spike the extremists' plans, I had three things to do.

First, I began a search among property agents throughout Central Scotland. Who was looking for utility property to rent short-term – possibly an isolated cottage but perhaps also a disused factory or warehouse building? Anyone of medium height or smaller, wearing steel-rimmed glasses? Or a man with a remarkable eagle-beak nose?

I was checking on a list of Edinburgh law firms when one of my mobile telephones rang. Since I was presumed to have perished in the Toyota crash, I had destroyed the telephone I was then carrying, and bought for cash a handful of pay-as-you-go instruments to throw away as soon as their available minutes were exhausted. Criminals, I understand, call such disposable instruments 'burners'.

I had of course ceased to use my bank card, relying now on funds placed long ago in Edinburgh for emergency. When I came back to life, it would have to be with a story of amnesia caused by injuries in the car smash.

The caller display on the new device showed a number that I did not know. Not even the dialling code was one that I recognized.

'This is Cameron MacKenzie'.

I knew the name. MacKenzie was with a firm of lawyers in Falkirk.

'I think we may have rented a property to one of the men about whom you were enquiring. A touch under medium height, wavy hair, steel-rimmed glasses?'

'That's right. What name did he give?'

'William Smith'.

Growing more and more inventive. Grant had been 'William Brown'.

'What sort of property?'

'Disused storerooms. Middle of Edinburgh. A bit hidden away, but somewhere quiet was what he said he wanted'.

'Rather out of your territory, isn't it?'

'Oh, it's part of a deceased's estate. Man had bits of property all over the place'.

'And the arrangements with this Smith?'

'Six months lease'.

'When was this fixed up?'

'About two weeks ago. Let me see. Seventeen days ago. This *is* the man you are interested in?'

'Sounds like him exactly'. I needed to have a look at this new place. 'Can you give me the address?'

'I can post you the details and a map showing how to get there. It's what we send to prospective tenants'.

'Can I have the address now?' I wanted nothing sent to Argyll, where I was believed dead, and should give my Edinburgh address to no one.

'Certainly'.

The location of the property looked to me absolutely ideal for the madmen's purpose. Along one of those broad back wynds with which Edinburgh is so well provided, but not a frequented one. Seven foot high walls on both sides along its entire length, guaranteeing maximum privacy to whatever businesses lay behind them. The property that 'Smith' had rented had double wooden gates swinging inwards into a generous yard. None of the neighbouring properties had the look or air of being in regular use. I walked the length of the wynd on a weekday evening. Not a light anywhere. The description of 'Smith' tallied, and to make sure, I photographed over the top of the gates. The storerooms had two windows, both boarded up. Not the sort of boards, either, that an owner uses to protect an unused building from run-of-the-mill vandalism. These were cut-down planks.

Experience had taught me the folly of being too easily satisfied. I parked on the opposite side of a street running along one end of the wynd, keeping an all-night watch along its length. The next night I repeated the procedure from a street at the other end. Alternating like this, I watched the place throughout most of the next four days and evenings. On the fifth morning, two men drove up to the double gates. One – MacNeb's curved nose was unmistakable – opened the gates. The car vanished into the yard. When I saw the photographs I had taken from behind my steering wheel, I was astonished at the images I had caught of MacNeb's companion. The resemblance to poor Dr Bruce was even clearer than I had seen when I first spotted the Lookalike among the crowd of shoppers at Aberfoyle. Damned near a dead ringer for the deceased doctor. Hair, as far as I could make out through windscreen glass, greying but certainly with the same waviness. Similar type of round face. Glasses unmistakably the same.

I had been prepared for a wait. No need. The Lookalike was ahead of me, had wasted no time, acted immediately after his loss of the cottage.

I had acquired copies of the plans of the premises, as lodged with Edinburgh Council. Examination of these confirmed that there was no way in or out except via the tall gates. Not satisfied with drawings that might be out of date, I went round to the street parallel to the wynd to examine the far side of the structure. As far as could be seen from outside, the layout corresponded to the architectural plans in every respect. No door or even a window at the back. Nothing in the way of an opening on that side among the neighbouring buildings, beyond a narrow gate some yards along from the back of the storerooms rented by 'Smith'.

That was the first issue settled.

The second thing I did was to have a word with some of my old Service colleagues, the strong-arm men we used to call goons. All retired now, and one, I discovered, the victim of a mild stroke. Three others, though, were fit and ready for anything. They were exactly the men I needed. None had heard of my supposed death. Could they spare a few days in Scotland in September, during the run-up to the referendum? I should cover their expenses and pay them for their efforts, as well.

One of these men I should place close to the SNP leader throughout the days immediately before polling stations opened. He would be near the leader as a bodyguard day and night, even though the man he was watching would not realize the fact. Any attempt to abduct the leader and blame this on Unionists would be snuffed out. I had confidence in my men, and in the event of the seizure succeeding should have the advantage of knowing precisely where it was intended to take the party leader.

XVII

NEXT, I set about tackling the most sensational of the plotters' schemes. If Grant had been able to research the previously unknown ancestry of a Westminster Minister, I should be able to do the same. Not, though, without the official status that I no longer possessed. Adoption agencies are notoriously secretive, and they slammed every figurative door directly in my face.

The fictional agent would of course have lost no time in seducing a woman employed by one of the adoption organizations. The information he required would have been in his hands before anyone could say: 'She'll never see *him* again'.

I could not behave like this. Nor, fortunately, did I need to. My Service training had taught me to open numerous types of lock. Acting from Berlin Station, I had accessed many of the other side's rooms and document cabinets.

Before burgling an adoption agency's office, I had to make a couple of assumptions. First, that while the details of present-day adoptions were carried on computer drives, those from the 1920s had not yet been transferred to computers, and were still stored in paper files. Secondly, that these old files were duplicated, that is, kept under the names of both the natural and the adoptive parents. Simple cross-referencing would therefore be possible. This being the case, searching under the surname of the Cabinet Minister's adoptive father should uncover at once the birth mother's name.

Scotland is not exactly littered with adoption agencies. I entered what I believed to be the oldest one, to find that the cabinet holding adoptive parents' names from the relevant part of the alphabet was not even locked. Four families with the right name were included, but one of the babies was a girl and none of the adoptions was dated within five years of the one I sought.

Letting myself out of the building, I all but bumped into a policeman. A copper on the beat! Where are any to be found, these days? And all alone, too! Health and Safety regulations drawn up in Brussels would doubtless like to keep them all safe in their stations, tied up doing paperwork, for fear that a burglar like myself might biff them one.

Rather than do that, of course, I wished 'Good night, officer'.

That was enough for one day. I saved the second address for the following night.

I went there well after midnight. They were awkward offices to access, but their filing cabinets were old and practically falling apart. A child could have been past the locks using only bare hands.

The records here were archived chronologically. Inside a minute I had in my hands not only the papers relating to the Bavarian girl's birth of a boy in Scotland, but also full data on the adoptive family whom the Cabinet Minister had grown up regarding as his grandparents.

Grant's instructions to his Nationalist cohorts were to release details of the birth and adoption, for maximum impact, two nights before the referendum.

230

My three goons arrived a week before polling day. MacDonald, a tough veteran newly retired to his home city of Inverness, was first to turn up. The other two, a Yorkshireman and a resident of the Home Counties, came a day later.

I quartered all three with me in the rooms that I had taken in Edinburgh, the base from which I had so far undertaken only nocturnal expeditions to adoption agencies.

Once my men were with me, one of them was to remain close to Scotland's First Minister at all times. Leaving them to sort out their own preferences in duty hours, I specified a round-the-clock rota of eight-hour shifts, beginning on the following day.

I began to think that I ought perhaps to have double the number, to have two men on watch at any time. Events were to prove this fear justified, but I was doubtful whether I could find so many retired goons fit and prepared to come and do what I asked. I consoled myself with the knowledge that the First Minister in any case had police protection. My men would be there as no more than reinforcement.

I distributed mobile phones between the four of us. There was no land line in my rooms, and I was going to have none connected.

Meanwhile, I had worked out the last detail that had puzzled me about the crash of the Toyota.

Nothing that I attempted could have prevented the smash. I had found myself in the position of the learner in a dual-control car when the instructor takes over. Driving had been taken out of my hands.

I knew exactly how this had been done, and my knowing was in itself a sheer fluke. I owed my knowledge to a tiny news item from last summer. In a short report, it was revealed that Volkswagen was suing the University of Birmingham because of research by some of its scientists. University computer experts had developed methods of hacking car anti-theft systems. Alongside VWs, Porsches and Audis they had found how to unlock even marques such as Lamborghini and Bentley.

Had I still been in the Service, news of this development would have had me initiating an investigation to see what we could use. I was still curious, and started a small inquiry of my own.

There were few secrets in the world of academic research, and I soon heard how American hackers had taken control of a car using a laptop computer. They had steered it and applied its brakes. That car was a Toyota.

The same men had disabled the brakes of a moving Ford using remote methods. They had even driven a car via a video game controller. These feats were accomplished by hacking into the cars' electronic control units via their on-board diagnostic ports. These electronic control units are part of the computer network that controls most functions of the modern car, including steering, braking, acceleration and even the horn. The American experts wrote software sending instructions through the diagnostic ports to override commands from the driver.

I can testify as to how well that works.

232

So much for the value of all those on-board computers built into our modern cars. Thankfully, my old E-Type, devoid of reliance on microchips, is immune from such interference. So too is my late mother's Vauxhall. Both were built before the computer craze.

How the loaned Toyota was taken from my control was no mystery. As I understood it, the hacker would need to do no more than lift the bonnet and download his own programme through the diagnostic port. With the car parked unprotected in my drive, access would be easy enough.

What I did not at first understand was how the hacker had triggered off his intervention at the riskiest spot in my journey. There was no doubt that I was intended to shoot off the road in that particular place. That was where steering had locked, brakes had failed and the engine had accelerated.

The hacker would have had to be a mind reader as well as an electronics wizard to know which route I intended to follow and to lie in wait with his box of tricks on the hillside above. There was no vehicle following me; I always keep an eye on my rear view mirrors and knew that I was alone on that road. From how far away, for goodness' sake, could the takeover of a car be activated? How, in any case, could the hacker know that I was approaching that particular hazard?

The solution came to me after some thought. GPS. The global positioning system used by millions of drivers to help them find their destinations. The software loaded into my diagnostic port will have included a database of potentially fatal road spots, along with code that triggered when the car reached one of these.

GPS, a friend to so many drivers, was the tool that had killed my poor passenger.

I had grossly underestimated MacNeb's technical knowhow and abilities. Or was it the Lookalike whose speciality was computer wizardry?

It was now Monday night. Less than two and a half days before polling stations were to open.

My goon MacDonald and I went separately to a major meeting addressed in Glasgow by the First Minister of Scotland, chief protagonist of the independence party. Though keeping well apart from each other, the two of us remained in positions from which we could intervene forcefully should any hostile move be made towards the country's leader.

Beyond the expected boisterousness, nothing happened. Knowing that at the conclusion of the gathering the First Minister would be shuffled away discreetly and swiftly via a side exit, I left the hall a little ahead of the crowd.

MacDonald stayed inside to oversee the First Minister leaving the platform. Adept at swift and unobtrusive movement, he was nonetheless close to the official car when a minute later it accelerated away with the nation's leader.

Both MacDonald and I were there to see the car glide up at BBC Scotland's headquarters on Pacific Quay. We did not speak to or otherwise acknowledge one another. The leader's journey had remained incident-free. With time until the referendum running short, his schedule was becoming more intense. On Wednesday he would be back at Pacific Quay for the final studio debate between himself and the very man at the head of the 'No' campaign whose ancestry it was planned to impugn.

In less than a half-hour, the leader's car was on the move again. Its destination was soon obvious. The leader was going home to Bute House, his official residence in Edinburgh, doubtless intending a good night's sleep ahead of the strenuous final two days of campaigning.

I found it surprising that in view of the technical sophistication available to them, Grant's pals had not shut down mobile phone communications in the region of Charlotte Square, the location of Bute House. As it was, MacDonald's message got through to me before the shooting started.

'Arrived Charlotte Square. Possible suspect car. Dark blue...'

The first shot came as I slid into the square. There was Robert Adam's elegant Bute House, there the First Minister's official car. One man, wearing steel-rimmed glasses, dragging the First Minister from the back seat by an arm.

A second, distinguished by a large curved nose, pointing an automatic pistol into the car interior. I slid my mother's Vauxhall to a halt, sprang out. MacNeb's second shot caught me in the right shoulder, ending my participation in the proceedings.

I heard the third and fourth shots, saw how the fourth slammed into MacDonald's leg as he came racing into view. Both of us down, and no, returning shots was not an option. MacNeb and the Lookalike were now forcing the First Minister across the road and into a dark blue car. They were practically smothering him. To have fired at either of the villains would have risked hitting the First Minister.

In any case, since leaving the Service, MacDonald no longer carried a firearm.

Shot three appeared to have disabled the First Minister's driver. The first I assumed to have put out of action the plain clothes man who guarded their passenger by sitting alongside him on the rear seat.

Two guards, no second car, no action from policemen on the ground.

Not any longer. After this, arrangements would definitely be beefed up to a sensible level.

Doors opened. Voices rose. Feet came running.

The First Minister was gone.

Only MacDonald and I knew where the dark blue car was taking him.

And we had both been shot.

XVIII

I PUSHED myself up and joined the group that had accumulated around MacDonald. He had been hit in the thigh, and was losing a lot of blood. His discipline remained superb. Even in those circumstances, he made no sound or gesture to indicate that we knew one another.

I returned to the Vauxhall and plucked my Burberry from the interior. Buttoning it half way was enough to cover the damage to my shoulder.

Police would be here at the touch of mobile phone buttons. Police meant questions. Plenty of them. How I knew what was going to happen, and how I chanced to be there when it did. Not for me. I had already been a suspect in Janine's abduction. That was enough.

All right, they had let me go on that one, but not, I couldn't help feeling, without some lingering suspicion and regret. And how was I to expound convincingly the plan to place public blame for the whole thing on Unionist 'No' campaigners? Once police were questioning me this time, I couldn't see myself walking out for at least a couple of days.

And in that couple of days a great deal was due to happen. I was not going to sit in a police station while acts preventable and damaging to our country were perpetrated unimpeded.

I took the Vauxhall out of Charlotte Square in discreet fashion. No need to attract attention. Fortunately, everyone was busy with MacDonald. The Lookalike and MacNeb, too, would be anxious not to attract unnecessary attention. They would hurry their car along briskly while avoiding anything spectacular. I imagined MacNeb sitting in the back seat pressing his gun barrel into the First Minister's ribs, while the Lookalike did the driving. Did the Lookalike, too, have a gun?

Two chaps with guns wouldn't worry James Bond. They certainly worried me. When they had our First Minister in their hands.

I could call in the police, give them the whereabouts of the storerooms and let their trained marksmen deal with the matter.

Like hell I could.

I was going to do this job myself. If I didn't, the real story of an attempt to blame the abduction on Unionists would be smothered by police bulletins. Not any fault of the police, of course. British police are always scrupulously fair, at all times conscientiously concerned to favour neither one side nor the other. They would announce that the First Minister had been abducted, that he had been released and that two men had been arrested (or shot). That would be it. No mention of any affiliation on the part of the two men, or of suspicion as to motives or political implications.

Normally, such impartiality and restraint would be fine. One could be sure that the full story would emerge in due course.

There was no time for that. This was Monday night. Referendum polling stations were due to open early Thursday morning. With outrageous anti-Unionist 'revelations' fresh and convincing in a shocked electorate's mind.

I called up both of my other goons, and set about following the car carrying the First Minister. The horsepower was there if I wanted it, but city streets were no place for a pursuit. There is a fundamental fact about chases that seems, inexplicably, to have escaped the forces of law and order. When someone knows that he is being chased, what does he do? What would you do? Quite right. You would go faster. And so does everyone else. Just what is needed in urban surrounddings, with pedestrians crossing streets, elderly people, mothers with pushchairs...

Law and order forces have no need to start a chase and put innocent people at risk. At their fingertips an organization waits for use. That organization can shadow any suspect vehicle, follow its progress, if necessary, from the air, and wait. Every motor has to stop some time. Once the driver pulls in for fuel, or when the tank runs dry, police may move in without exposing surrounding public to danger. Time works for the law and order men. All they need is patience. Except in cases where it is necessary to catch the suspect before he can throw incriminating material from the car, and that sort of thing.

Aware of all this, I held back from racing after the car with the First Minister. I let it disappear behind the twin gates in the wynd, confident that with the assistance of my two men I could free the country's leader without any injury to him.

I switched off my lights on entering the wynd, stopped my engine half way along, and glided in close alongside those two gates. No one was going to drive out of there. The lights of my two goons' car went out as soon as they touched one end of the wynd. The motor died, and I saw my men start around the corner towards me. Black from the feet up, they slid along close to the seven foot walls in something near to invisibility.

I climbed onto the bonnet of the Vauxhall, pulled myself to the top of the gates, dropped over. In the yard, the dark blue car. Beyond that, blackness. No light from the storerooms. Nothing sophisticated securing the big doors to the building. Just an ordinary mortice lock.

I had not realized this before breaking my neck, but in order to look into something below ordinary eye level it is necessary to bend to the appropriate height, then tilt one's head back. I can turn my neck left and right fully, but have difficulty tipping my head back. I sank down into my fully bent knees like one of those Russian dancers. My eyes were now at the right level. I slipped my magic tool into the lock.

Two shotgun blasts ended the peace of the wynd. A booby trap aimed straight at the face of a tamperer standing normally. Whoever set those gun barrels had not anticipated a low-level picklock.

The blasts gave me a sizeable hole in one of the doors. That hole gave me a useful grip. Livid, I flung myself onto it.

Inside the storerooms, a massive crash. A motorcycle engine started up. grew louder, zoomed away to the left.

'Damn'.

I had been through bigger setbacks, and so far none had pushed me beyond 'damn'. Still had a ridiculous image of Anna being close and able to overhear, I suppose. Or my mother.

My goons vaulted over into the yard.

'Get out and round to the back'.

The faster man clambered back into the wynd. The motorbike sound was disappearing.

Entrance façade and back wall of the building were of brick. What I could not have envisaged was that its side walls were wooden. The elderly structures facing on to this wynd had been erected in a period of austerity. At the time, decently solid wood had doubtless sufficed for buildings that were for the most part cheek by jowl. Through one side wall a crude pre-cut doorway had been battered out from the inside. On the floor lay a sledgehammer, instrument of that almighty crash. What a find this building must have been for the Lookalike and MacNeb. An escape route right to hand. They were all ready to take off when necessary, but surely could not have anticipated being forced so quickly into a retreat. On their way on their motorbike as soon as they knew that the booby trap was keeping no one out.

Frankly, I should have expected them to stay and start shooting. Presumably they imagined a huge posse of police outside. As fanatics, of course, they would not want to be collared or downed until they had completed the programme left to them by the dead Grant.

That 'damn' of mine had not been enough, I knew, but I wasn't going to say any more. I had examined the building front and back, and given no attention to its sides. The official plans told me that there were no side openings, and with properties close on either flank, this was perforce the case. The Lookalike and MacNeb had made their own opening, ridden through it into the backyard of an adjacent building, and surely exited via the narrow gate out of there. I had seen that confounded gate while examining the far side of the storerooms, and thought nothing of it because it belonged to other premises. The men's getaway was all my fault. Still, I knew where I had to go to frustrate the last of their knavish tricks.

For now, our concern had to be the welfare of the First Minister. We found him behind a steel door, shocked by the sound of shotgun fire, angry, ready to give us a memorable sample of his politician's best eloquence. Had we not come to free him, I'm sure he would have made us feel quite ashamed.

Being locked in a self-contained interior storeroom, the First Minister was unable to take advantage of the hole made in the side wall. The room that held him had a narrow single bed made up in a corner. Along an opposite wall, a line of steel filing cabinets was topped with tins of meat, new potatoes, soup and other victuals. A gas ring and saucepan stood on a desk, with several crates of spring water on the floor. Connecting doors led to an obvious manager's office and beyond that a WC. Since this building housed storerooms, it had been much easier barricading in the First Minister than it would have been at the cottage used for the experimental abduction of Janine.

'I can't understand it', the First Minister complained, once he realized our good intentions. 'They are my own supporters'.

'You recognized them?'

'Both of them. They were in my party'.

'Were?'

'We had to throw them out. They were extremists. When all the opinion polls showed that we had no hope of winning with a 'yes' vote, they wanted to use weapons to achieve independence. Totally lunatic, of course. How on earth did they think that we could ever take on United Kingdom forces, even if all the Scottish regiments sided with us? In any case, we are pacifists'.

The First Minister shook his head. 'And now they do a thing like this? Why?'

'To throw the blame on the *No* campaign. Something simpler, and less risky, than using weapons'.

'They took away my mobile phone'.

Yes. Had they left him with it, and he used it, police would have determined his location in no time at all.

The goon who had run round to the back came panting in through the ragged doorway from the adjacent yard. The narrow gateway onto the road behind, he reported, had been locked but was smashed open. Of course. It was just the width to allow a motorcycle through. My man had seen nothing of the escaping machine, but described a narrow alleyway leading away on the opposite side of the road, too narrow for a car but well wide enough for a motorcycle. The Lookalike and MacNeb had had their exit wonderfully well prepared.

Inside two more minutes my men had the tall gates opened and the First Minister seated in the back of my Vauxhall. Meanwhile, I was calling my contact on the news desk at the BBC.

'How far have you got with the First Minister story?'

'Ian! You're supposed to be dead'.

'A mistake. Don't give the game away until after the referendum, and I'll let you have the exclusive story'.

'It's a deal. There's total chaos here. How much do you know about this First Minister thing?'

'I can tell you this: the man is free again'.

'What?'

'And in my car. I'll call you later. And stand by for one of my men bringing documents'.

No point trying to take the First Minister back to Bute House. The whole of Charlotte Square would be swarming with uniforms. 'Crime scene' tape all over the place. And all round nothing but one-way signs. I drove half way along North Castle Street, and left it at that.

'Off you go, and don't let it happen again'. The First Minister was not amused. All the same, he set off smartly enough along the shortest path towards Bute House. He would enjoy telling his story, that was sure. Not least on television. Ought to bring his 'Yes' campaign another half million votes, he was probably telling himself. Should be surprised, though, if he could tell anyone where he had been.

I should be giving everything to the police, of course. First, though, I was going to see that the BBC had the full and correct story. I also needed to place photocopies of certain documents into the hands of one of Her Majesty's Ministers.

After that, there was only one further matter to be addressed.

XIX

NO mystery about where I had turned the First Minister out of my car. CCTV from North Castle Street would have done more than confirm his story. It would also have revealed my Vauxhall's number plate.

Good luck to police raiding my Argyll home.

There would be teams combing Edinburgh's hotels, too, and it would be cruel of me to leave them long on this fruitless exercise.

Once I had settled the last of this business, I should be off into the nearest hospital for attention to my shoulder. That would bring them running.

Now that the First Minister was safe, my first concern was MacDonald's condition.

Ringing round the hospitals, though, not such a good idea. No faster way to attract suspicions than enquiring after a gunshot victim. Except for immediate family, of course.

I called my BBC contact.

'What do you know about any shootings this evening?'

'One guy dead, two in hospital'.

'Dead chap in the First Minister's car?'

'That's right'.

'And the other two?'

'One serious body wound. Not sure where. One bullet in thigh. Okay, I believe'.

That was what I needed to know.

In response I confirmed that I was sending round one of my goons with full details of the scheme for abducting the First Minister and framing the 'No' campaigners.

In addition, ancestry data for the leading 'No' protagonist. Birth certificates of his grandfather, of both his grandfather's parents, adoption papers, everything.

'Thanks a lot, Ian. I owe you a big one on this. Let's get together for that long overdue drink without leaving it very much longer'.

I acquiesced in general terms, and rang off. I wasn't going to meet anyone while I still had a bullet in my shoulder.

No one was going to whip me off into a hospital while there were still things to do.

All that mattered to me was that the referendum result should not be influenced by anyone prepared to stoop to dirty tricks, let alone to murder.

That idiotic 'fifty per cent plus one' was disturbing me.

Really ought to see about heading back home, to get my own vote in.

Suppose I were the one whose failure to cast his vote made all the difference?

Was all that only one night ago?

Now, the night before the final day's referendum campaigning, the Nationalist plotters were left with only one piece of skulduggery in their armoury. It remained for me to thwart this. Rain-soaked in my dark corner, I lifted my arm. If I didn't start to move it about, it would go stiff on me.

Before I could begin preventive isometrics, a mobile phone call came in. One of my two unwounded goons.

'Sir, those two on the motorbike. They ran smack into a whisky lorry down by Leith docks'.

'Are they...?'

'Yes. Both dead'.

Good. No vanload of explosives to wait for, after all. Yet just where was the van? They hadn't kept it on the premises where they took the First Minister. Presumably they were heading off to collect it when they had their smash. Stored down by Leith docks, then? Wherever the van was, we needed to locate it and disarm the load before some accidental detonation.

I should do no good standing here. I stepped out from my corner, shook some of the rain off my coat and took a step towards the only road leading to and from where I had waited.

MacNeb and the Lookalike might be out of the picture, but here came someone else, winding up a motor through the gears, going for the slope. I stepped back from the approach road.

Its sides close enough for me to reach out and touch, a white van burst onto the enclosed space that was the road's dead end. A flash as the cab swept beneath the overhead lighting. An instant only, but it was enough to see the dark hair still thick on both sides of a shining bare pate. Light blue eyes. A profile I had known for years.

How things ended that Tuesday night I prefer not to discuss. Description is perhaps best left to the official reports.

Whichever newspaper version you pick up is as inaccurate as any other:

'*According to eyewitnesses, among them many foreign tourists, a white van, driven in orderly fashion along the Royal Mile, accelerated sharply on approaching Edinburgh Castle Esplanade. It headed at top speed across the 140 yards of the Esplanade towards the guarded main entrance to the castle.*

'*When the van was about half way across, the driver baled out and rolled away from the vehicle in paratrooper landing style. The driverless van continued on at speed directly towards the castle entrance, where two Scots soldiers stood on guard duty. The vehicle would undoubtedly have hit the gateway and killed the guards, but for the courageous and self-sacrificing action of a Deputy Chief Constable of Scotland's police. The officer, who is yet to be named, flung himself into the driver's cab and detonated the explosives with which the van had been jampacked, before it could reach the men on guard.*

'*An intense police search is now under way for the driver of the deadly vehicle, who after baling out of his cab was able to escape in the general confusion*'.

News of the explosion was broadcast without attribution to either side. The occurrence was treated as a mystery.

That was the end not only of the plot to defame Unionists but also of the remaining Nationalist conspirator. Why Nick did not use remote means to send in the van and detonate its load, I can only speculate. My guess is that the necessary electronic control was in the possession of one of the dead pair.

Nick had sprung into the breach immediately on hearing of their smash – a well-concealed fanatical agent who must have orchestrated the various attempts on my life after seeing that confusion over 'Poles' failed to end my digging into Dr Bruce's death. You will of course form your own view, but I cannot regret the bullet that had detonated the load in the van. It had ended Nick's effort to roll away, bringing him a posthumous medal rather than the prison term he deserved, but it had saved the guardsmen.

Naturally, I had already placed in the hands of the Cabinet Minister whose grandparentage had finally been established copies of the same birth and adoption documents that I had handed to the BBC. That done, I was satisfied that reproductions of these papers would reach all branches of the media alongside the fraudulent copies produced by Grant. The key to Grant's plan lay in not giving press and television details of the adopted baby's fatherhood until two days before the independence referendum, so that the story would dominate the final day's campaigning. 'Doesn't matter' said Grant as he lay dying, meaning that once polling stations had closed and the electorate given its irrevocable voice, the truth would be, as he also said, 'too late'.

My BBC friend called me back. 'We've had that grandfather story sent to us - anonymously'.

'Naturally', I told him. 'It's all in the timing. You are meant to come out with it on your news right now, just in time to shock the *Don't knows* into becoming *Yes* supporters. Even switch a few *No*s over to *Yes*, as well'.

And it would have done. The birth certificate originating from Grant, naming the father of the Bavarian girl's boy as Adolf Hitler, had been forged with considerable skill.

The Minister's real grandfather was a Scotsman who had died in a work accident in Canada. His pregnant widow had returned to Scotland. After giving birth to their baby boy, she suffered a breakdown and could not cope. A letter in the mother's file showed that doctors had persuaded her to let the infant be adopted. All perfectly respectable.

Referendum Day came and went, ending with that unforgettable broadcast announcement:

'The numbers of votes cast were as follows...'

THE BOOK STOPS HERE